DEEP COVER
THE UNKNOWING AGENT

JEFFREY JAY LEVIN

Black Rose Writing | Texas

ISBN: 978-1-68513-436-5
PUBLISHED BY BLACK ROSE WRITING
www.blackrosewriting.com

Printed in the United States of America
Suggested Retail Price (SRP) $18.95

Deep Cover is printed in Garamond Premier Prot

*As a planet-friendly publisher, Black Rose Writing does its best to eliminate unnecessary waste to reduce paper usage and energy costs, while never compromising the reading experience. As a result, the final word count vs. page count may not meet common expectations.

PRAISE FOR
DEEP COVER

"Levin delivers a twisty, action-packed story of deep-cover Russian spies that plays on long-time fears and rumors. As the tension amps up, we don't know who to trust."
–Lena Gibson, award-winning author of *The Wish* and *The Edge of Life*

"*Deep Cover* is a Cold War thriller that takes place over fifty years. A long forgotten Soviet Spy program is reactivated and it is no longer clear who the bad guys are. Stephan Beck finds himself fighting not just for his life, but also to prevent a war with Russia. Jeff Levin will keep you guessing until the final pages of this international thriller."
–Gary Gerlacher, author of *Faulty Bloodlines*

"This one reads like a classic Hollywood paranoia thriller writ large! The fingernail-shredding climax will test every square inch of your nerves. *Deep Cover* is supremely entertaining."
–David Buzan, author of *In the Lair of Legends*

For Shani, Jessica, Aiden and Liana:
Dreams Become Reality

To Alexis: For continuing to put up with a possessed/obsessed writer

DEEP COVER

"He that can have patience, can have what he will."
–Benjamin Franklin

INTRODUCTION

1975

"Idyllic," was the only word that came to Peter Jones' mind as he drove his one-year-old navy blue Chevy Impala through the quiet streets of his town. As he slowly drove home, careful not to exceed the posted speed limit of 30 miles per hour, he passed many neighbors out enjoying the sunny day. They were mowing and watering carefully manicured lawns, throwing balls to dogs anxiously anticipating a retrieval dash, and playing catch, languidly tossing balls to and fro. Recognizing some, he waved through his open window as he passed. At the park, a little league baseball game was in full swing and he took a moment while observing the "Stop" sign to watch the kids chasing the ball as if attempting to catch a pack of wild rabbits. Laughing, he drove on. It was the 4th of July and it was looking as if it would be just grand, like an updated version of the fictional Mayberry.

He pulled into the driveway of his 2 bedroom, 1½ bath ranch style home, and remarked to himself that it was fortuitous he had memorized the number of the house, so prominently displayed next to the front door, as each of the houses had nearly identical exteriors, save for a different color or planting here and there. After stepping out of the driver's seat, he paused to observe his surroundings and take a deep breath of fresh, clean air. He sighed with satisfaction as he opened the back door and removed two bags of groceries, cradling them in his arms as he approached the unlocked front door.

He entered the house to sounds of the Bee Gees *Jive Talkin* coming from the hi-fi in the living room. The music masked his entry, allowing him to covertly approach the kitchen, where his wife, Roxanne Jones, an attractive 25-year-old brunette, with high cheekbones and a thin nose, was cutting lettuce near the sink. He secretly gazed at her seductive figure outlined by her snug red and blue skirt and tight-fitting white blouse. She stood amidst bowls brimming with lettuce, adding freshly cut vegetables to them. Sensing a new presence, she spun around with knife in hand to find Peter gaping at her in surprise.

"Whoa there," he blurted out while using his bags of groceries as a shield.

Relaxing at the sight of him, she lowered the knife and reached for one of the bags, leaning in for a quick kiss as she did so.

"I was beginning to wonder if you were ever coming home," she remarked.

He walked to the only clear counter space and began emptying his grocery bag of hamburger buns, hot dog buns, and bags of potato chips. "It's the 4th of July and, believe it or not, we are not the only people having a barbeque," he said. "The store was an absolute madhouse."

Not looking up from her chores, she replied, "I'll take care of that. Please get the grill started. People will be here soon."

Dutifully, he said, "Yes, ma'am," as he headed out the sliding glass door to the waiting grill.

•   •   •

Peter, Roxanne, and their friends and neighbors were drinking beer and wine at an outdoor picnic table set on a red brick patio surrounded by tiki torches. They were joined by Greg and Susan Williams, both 26 years old, James Wilson, 25, and his stunningly beautiful wife Linda, 26. Greg was a short, portly man and his wife was an average-looking woman in all respects. James, as if paired with his wife by a matchmaker, was a tall, muscular man who could easily pass as an NFL quarterback. The detritus of the meal littered the table as the men and woman were each engaged in conversation within their respective group.

Peter, rather emphatically, stated, "We could've won that damn war if we'd only sent more troops! We've *never* lost a war. It's a damn disgrace, is what it is."

Greg, with somewhat less passion, replied, "We could've sent all the troops in the world and not won that thing. It was an un-winnable situation. Better we get the hell out of there and save some lives."

James, not to be left out, chimed in, "I don't know. I think we could've done something. It's those damn hippies and the media that turned public opinion around. All you have to do is look at their hair to know they were up to no-good. Bunch of commies, is what I think. If we could've controlled that situation, I think we could've had a better outcome."

Having heard the tone of the men's conversation, Roxanne turned to her husband and asked, "Are you arguing about that damn war again?"

"Not arguing. Civilly discussing," was Peter's response.

"It's a fine line," she retorted.

"We're managing to walk the tightrope," responded James.

"And that 'damn war', as you put it," continued Peter, his voice rising, "could be an enormous problem. You've heard of the domino effect? Once Vietnam goes, the rest of Asia will follow. Then we'll really have our hands full with those damn commies!"

At the increase in both tone and volume, the women ceased their conversation and turned to the rest of the group. Seeing this, and feeling just a little foolish, Peter raised his hands in mock surrender and apologized. "Sorry, I know I have a tendency to get a little riled up."

"That you do," said Roxanne. She arose from her chair and continued, "Let's have dessert."

Gathering the dirty plates and silverware, the other women joined her as the men ignored the chores and began discussing football.

•   •   •

Later that evening, after their guests had gone home, Roxanne and Peter were in the kitchen, where Peter was actually helping Roxanne clean up.

"Thanks for helping, Pete."

"Glad to pitch in."

"I had a nice evening. How about you?" asked Roxanne.

Putting down his dish towel, Peter approached Roxanne and took her in his arms. "I did. Thank you."

As Roxanne put her arms around Peter's neck, she let a little kiss transform into a much more passionate embrace. As Peter lowered his hands to cup his wife's tightly clad buttocks, she pressed against him and whispered into his ear, "Take me to bed."

Not having to be told twice, he led her towards the bedroom, both shedding layers of clothing as they proceeded. As they approached the bedroom door, now both nearly naked, Peter whisked Roxanne off her feet and maneuvered through the bedroom door, kicking it closed behind him. Hastily removing whatever undergarments remained attached to their bodies, they fell onto the bed, Roxanne under Peter. Spreading her legs as Peter arranged himself on top of her, she whispered into his ear once again.

"Pyotya. Ya Hochyoo Eemyetz Staboy Re ebyonka!"

Too excited to have registered what he had just heard, he entered her as they vigorously made love. Moments later, the bedroom door reacted violently to the hard rubber sole of a black boot, spraying wood splinters into the room as it swung wildly on its hinges and crashed into the wall behind it.

Storming into the room before either Roxanne or Peter could react, Colonel Leonid Pushkin rushed to the bed, grabbed Peter by the shoulder, and flung him to the floor, just as Peter was in the throes of climax, sending his seed flying across the room. Too stunned to react, and being fully aware of his place in the hierarchy of life, Peter lie on the floor as Pushkin grabbed Roxanne by the right arm as she futilely attempted to cover her bare breasts with her left. With his free hand, he slapped her across both cheeks, first with a forehand, followed closely by a backhand, sending spittle and blood following Peter's wasted semen.

Fuming, he hissed, "English! How many times have I told you, only English?!?"

Too stunned to respond, and recognizing a rhetorical question when she heard it, she wisely elected to stay silent, except for the deep sobs which she was powerless to stop.

Turning to the door, where Captain Yuri Ovechkin silently observed the proceedings, Pushkin shoved Roxanne towards his inferior as he spat, "Take her to the treatment room." Captain Ovechkin silently nodded his assent as Pushkin stormed from the room, still obviously agitated.

•　　•　　•

As he left the house and entered his waiting UAZ-469, Colonel Pushkin visibly relaxed as a hint of an ironic smile touched his lips. The smile was brought about by his recollection of his own life. As he drove, he reflected on his upbringing and the hard lessons learned as a child, one specific lesson in particular.

•　　•　　•

Leonid Pushkin was born during a bitterly cold snap in 1940. Russia was deeply involved in the Second World War, so his father, an officer in the Russian infantry, was at the front on the day of his birth, trying to keep warm and alive. This he had in common with the rest of his now growing family. Leonid's mother, accompanied by her cousin and a local mid-wife, gave birth in a room heated only by a coal stove, which was not enough to stop the frozen billowing cloud which was her breath from floating into the room with each scream. The lives of mother and child during that time and in that place were tenuous at best, so it was something of a miracle that both had survived.

Home life while Papa was away was difficult, with food and coal being in short supply. Miraculously, his father survived the war and came home to his wife and son when Leonid was about six years old, only to find living conditions almost as difficult as in the field. The family's fortunes, however, were about to improve greatly. Having survived the war, and having been an officer, Papa was in position to be promoted in the field and, shortly after arriving home, posted to Moscow as an officer in the relatively new People's Commissariat for

State Security (NKGB). In Leonid's eyes, Papa was a genuine hero, if for nothing else, providing a warm home, comfortable bed, and food to eat. If Leonid had believed in super heroes, his father would have been flying around the apartment with a red cape emblazoned with the hammer and sickle symbol. Love shone from the boy's eyes each time he looked at his beloved Papa.

Lieutenant Alexi Pushkin, like many soldiers throughout the violent history of life, had a difficult time adjusting to what was, ostensibly, civilian life. He came back a different person from the idealistic young man who first left to fight for his country. He still had that nationalistic fervor, fueled by the loud and vigorous rhetoric of Joseph Stalin, but, without the war, he was uncertain how to pursue what he had truly come to love: the fight. And now, this little human followed him around whenever he could, clinging to his legs and staring at him with what his wife told him, was adoration. It was all just a little too much for the Lieutenant. Thankfully for him, he had the NKGB, which provided the dual solace of a place to escape to, as well as a fight, although not as out in the open as he was accustomed to during the war. He dove into his new assignment as if his life depended on it, which, over time, he came to realize, it did. And he was very good at it.

As Leonid got older, he developed a certain curiosity. An only child, he was often alone while his parents had some private time, and he took to quietly leaving his room to crouch outside his parent's bedroom, his ear to the door. In this way, he became privy to portions of otherwise private discussions about certain political matters, people under suspicion by the NKGB, and, strangely, noises that he just could not identify, which only made him more curious, and, perhaps, a little careless. It was on one such occasion that he inadvertently bumped the door, not making a lot of noise, but just enough. Frozen in place in an effort to magically disappear, he discovered that invisibility wasn't an option as the bedroom door was thrust open and his father, covered only in a sheet, loomed over him, grabbed him by the scruff of his neck, hauled him to his feet, and, after dragging Leonid to his own bedroom, made the boy intimately acquainted with the elder Pushkin's leather belt.

As Leonid later discovered, his father wasn't all that upset by the fact of his snooping. He was more upset that Leonid was careless and got caught. It was a lesson Leonid kept with him throughout his life.

.   .   .

He remembered that particular lesson with a strange fondness as he drove through the streets of the unnamed fake town, out past its boundaries, and through an overly large overhead door into the cold sunshine of the Siberian countryside. Once outside the building, he drove further on and upwards to the crest of a hill approximately two kilometers from the door through which he had just passed. He exited the vehicle and climbed up the hill to get a view of the enormous building. The building covered an area of almost five square kilometers and had a high-security fence around it. Stretching, he gazed skyward as he thought to himself, "I hope this doesn't turn into yet another fiasco of our esteemed leadership."

NATIONAL RECONNAISSANCE OFFICE HEADQUARTERS
CHANTILLY, VIRGINIA
1975

The National Reconnaissance Office (NRO) had been established on August 25, 1960. The mission was to develop, build, launch, and operate space reconnaissance systems and conduct intelligence-related activities for U.S. national security.

Housed in a large, nondescript gray building, to the uninformed it would appear to be a large warehouse or distribution facility. To the informed, it was a major component of the national security for the United States of America.

In a large windowless room located on the first of five lower levels of the building, in which special sound shielding had been built into the thick concrete walls, numerous work stations and large conference tables competed with a few small desks for space. On most of the tables and work stations were light tables and x-ray view boxes. Clamped to each viewing surface was a portable magnifier, under which were various photographic images taken from either satellites or spy planes. At work in the room were two dozen men and one woman. All the people in the room were in their late 20s or early 30s and, except for two of the men, they wore conservative civilian clothes. The two not dressed in civilian clothes were attired in military uniforms. USAF Lt. Daniel Fowler, a well-muscled 33-year-old, and USAF Sgt. Robert Ferguson, an equally well trimmed 28-year-old. Each was hunched over a light table as they looked through a large magnifier, under which was a photograph of an enormous building, which was part of a compound located inside a high security fence somewhere in Siberia. Visible on the road leading into the compound was a convoy of various trucks, a combination of both military and civilian semi-trailers.

"That building is enormous. How have we not been able to figure out what it is?" a frustrated Lt. Fowler inquired of Sgt. Ferguson.

"It is, apparently, a very well-guarded secret. Our best guesses, to date, have been a warehouse or factory of some sort," Sgt. Ferguson replied.

"If it's a factory, I think we'd see smoke billowing from smokestacks. If it's a warehouse, why is it located so remotely and so well guarded?" commented the Lieutenant, almost as if speaking to himself. Turning to his companion, he surmised, "Unless it's a weapons warehouse or research facility of some sort."

In response, the Sargent merely shrugged.

Using a sharpened pencil as a pointer and aiming it at the picture, Lt. Fowler asked, "What about these trucks? Have we been able to backtrack where they're coming from? Some look like civilian rigs. We should be able to bribe somebody."

"We did have somebody snooping around for information. He was found face down in the Moskva River two days ago."

Visibly perturbed by the realization that he had not yet been advised of this fact, Lt. Fowler quickly turned on his Sargent. "Why the hell am I just hearing about this now?"

"The information came in about an hour ago while you were out. I just haven't had a chance to bring it up." Seeing that his superior officer was not yet mollified, he continued, "Sorry."

Having received the apology, the Lieutenant visibly relaxed and returned his gaze to the photograph. He tapped the picture with the pencil and said, "If this is worth killing over, we really need to find out what it is." Turning to face Sargent Ferguson, he said, "Set up a meeting with the Colonel."

Taken aback by this statement, the Sargent asked, "Are you sure you want to do that at this juncture?"

"If we're going to expend more men and resources into this investigation, we're going to need his authorization. Set it up."

Resignedly, Sgt. Ferguson replied, "Yes, sir."

•　　　•　　　•

The "Colonel" was Colonel Horatio Castle, a career member of the USAF. One does not generally rise through the ranks to such heights without an exemplary career, and Colonel Castle was no exception. Dressed in his uniform, complete with a chest full of medals, standing at his full six foot, three inches, his square-jawed face posed an intimidating façade, a fact of which he was all too conscious and which he frequently used to his advantage.

Being "The Colonel," his schedule was filled, and would have been if a week consisted of eight days. Consequently, it was a full two weeks before Lt. Fowler was able to obtain an audience with his superior. With the extra two weeks, the Lieutenant and his team were able to gather more information and pictures, which proved valuable.

Admitted to the Colonel's large, plush office at the appointed time on the appointed day, Lt. Fowler, carrying a briefcase, approached the large ornately decorated wooden desk, behind which the Colonel was seated. Having reached the desk, he stood at attention and saluted. The Colonel, studying some pictures on his desk through a magnifying glass which was attached to a stand, looked up and casually returned the salute as he returned his attention to the photos.

"Have a seat, Dan."

Relaxing, Lt. Fowler replied, "Thank you, sir," as he sat in one of the two waiting chairs facing the desk. He placed the briefcase on the floor, within easy reach, removed his cap, placed it on his lap, and quietly waited.

The Colonel, having completed his perusal of the picture, exhibited it to Lt. Fowler as he stated, "This is quite the facility. What the hell is it?"

"We're not sure, just yet. We've had our people making some discreet inquiries, but there is a tight, seemingly leakproof seal surrounding anything that may be related to it."

"With that kind of security, it must be important."

"We think so as well, sir." Reaching down for his briefcase, Lt. Fowler continued. "We have been able to glean one bit of information, which I think you will find most interesting."

"What might that be, Dan?"

Removing a black-and-white photograph from his briefcase, Lt. Fowler quickly glanced at it before he passed it to the Colonel.

The Colonel reached for it, placed it on his desk and stared intently, without saying a word. The Lieutenant returned the silence.

After what seemed an eternity, the Colonel looked up and practically spat his next word.

"Pushkin."

The Colonel's face and tense body language revealed an intense hatred.

"Yes, sir. He must have gone out, stopped on that hill and looked up, just as the satellite moved into position. A lucky break for us."

Returning his attention to the photograph, Colonel Castle said, without looking up, "That shit-eating-grin makes me think he knew the damn satellite was there."

Lt. Fowler chose this moment to press his advantage. "If Pushkin is personally involved in this, it may be even more important than we believed."

The Colonel tore his gaze from the photo and brought his attention back to Lt. Fowler. "Whatever you need, Lieutenant, you've got it. I want to know what this bastard's up to."

Trying to hide a shit-eating-grin of his own, the Lieutenant responded, "I'm a bit curious, myself, sir."

RUSSIA
EARLY 1976

The sheer size of the compound made it impossible to hide it completely from the ground, even though it had been painted white for the winter. The white exterior, including the roof, was considerably more effective from the air, which was the Russian's primary concern.

Having become aware of the U.S. satellite schedule, they planned truck deliveries for those times when the unseen sky above was free of foreign eyes. This being one of those times, a convoy of trucks was approaching on the snow covered road. As the procession approached, two small mounds of what appeared to be snow moved on a hillside about a mile away. One mound was a white camouflaged Alexi Kutsovich, a thirty-year-old native Russian, and the other was his wife Tamara, also thirty-years-old and a native, similarly clothed. Alexi held a pair of state-of-the-art high-powered binoculars to his eyes and focused on the approaching trucks. Tamara held a notepad and pen, ready to transcribe what her husband called out.

"Shestz Polu Traktorov, Byez Peechyatse. Nyee Veezhu namyera attsyuda. Tree Vayenich Trasporta. Zakritiyeah. (Six semis, civilian, no markings. I can't make out the tag numbers from here. Three military transports, covered.)"

As Tamara took notes, Alexi spotted a dark colored Mercedes coming down a side road toward the compound gate and instantly turned his head, together with the binoculars, in its direction, a flash of sunlight momentarily reflecting off the lens.

"Eto Gasoodarstveeniy eelee krootoy v ayeniy (That's got to be a government or military big shot)" commented Alexi.

"Navyerna KGB. Payehalee obratno. (More likely KGB. Maybe we should head back)," was Tamara's response.

Not wanting to pass on this opportunity, Alexi said, "Nyee shays. Davay Posmontrim Kto V'M ashine. (Not yet. Let's see if we can see who's in that car.)"

Watching, the two stayed perfectly still, having practiced disappearing into the surroundings over many hours. As the car approached the main building, Alexi slowly reached next to him and pulled out a camera with a long telephoto lens from the well-hidden bag. Trading the binoculars for the camera, he took picture after picture, the speed winder making a slight whirring sound as it wound the film. He did this until the car disappeared through the large, closing, overhead door.

Nervously, Tamara whispered, "Ya Doomayoo Ooytsee (I think we should go now.)"

Nodding his head in agreement, her husband said, "Saglasyeen. (I agree.)"

Carefully placing their equipment into the bag at Alexi's side, they put their gloves on and slowly slithered backwards in an effort to remain hidden. As they did so, a whining sound became audible from behind them, as if an enormous swarm of bees was approaching. Instead, they recognized it for what it was. Snowmobiles.

"Anyee Obnorhuzilye! Byeegee! (They've found us! Run!)" was Tamara's reaction, as she began to follow her own directions.

Hissing his response, he said, "Nyet! V'Snigoo! Bistra! (No! Get down into the snow!)"

Either not having heard or in too much of a panic to listen, Alexi could only watch as Tamara continued her attempted escape.

"Blydz! (Shit!)"

Removing a glove, he reached into a pocket of his heavy coat and withdrew a pistol as he attempted to catch-up with Tamara, just as three snowmobiles crested the hill behind him. Seeing what he determined would be his best chance, he stood his ground, took a shooter's stance and fired two rounds, each hitting the lead rider in the chest and sending the machine tumbling off course. The element of surprise having been erased, the remaining riders took evasive action as they returned fire, hitting Alexi in the leg. Seeing what had happened to her husband, Tamara rushed to his side, where they were quickly overtaken by the remaining snowmobile riding soldiers, as the otherwise pristine snow was dyed red with Alexi's blood.

•　　•　　•

Colonel Pushkin paced casually in front of Alexi and Tamara, both of whom were bound to uncomfortable chairs. Visible bruises appeared on Alexi's face and exposed chest, while blood still dripped from his wounded leg. Tamara appeared unhurt, but very distressed, unable to reach out for her husband. To this point in the interrogation, no questions had yet been posed to the couple. Leaning casually against a wall and observing the proceedings was Captain Ovechkin.

In a calm, conversational tone, Colonel Pushkin said, "Nu Alexi, Shot Ti Stvayey Abayatceelnay Zhinoy Preeyehol V'Seeber Shyaz? (So, Alexi, what brings you and your lovely wife to Siberia this time of year?)"

No response was forthcoming, so the Colonel continued, unperturbed, "Ya Oogadal shto ti eescheez haroshovo myesta dlye penceeyi? Nyet? (Let me guess, you were looking for a nice, quiet place to retire. No?)"

Not offering a response, a defiant Alexi lifted his head and glared at his tormentor.

"Perhaps you'd understand better if I spoke in English. After all, you are working for the Americans."

Moving impossibly quickly, Pushkin stepped forward and slapped Alexi hard across the face, sending spittle and blood flying onto a horrified Tamara. A furious Pushkin screamed into his captive's face, "Traitor!"

Standing and retreating a step, Pushkin calmed himself as he strolled to a table on which were displayed the clothing and gear taken from his guests. As he inspected the table's contents, he nonchalantly said, "This is very nice, and very expensive, equipment." Turning to face Alexi, he said, "I wonder how you could afford it." After a brief pause, he continued, "Don't bother trying to explain. I think I know the answer already." Pacing back and forth in front of both Alexi and Tamara, he glanced at Captain Ovechkin and continued, "It seems that our American friends have taken an interest in our little facility here."

Stopping in front of Tamara, he leaned over and gently caressed Tamara's face. "That's really too bad for the both of you."

Leaving a trembling Tamara, the Colonel stepped in front of Alexi, whose head was again slumped against his chest. Lifting his head by the hair, Pushkin stared into Alexi's face and said, "It's also too bad for you that, two days ago, your friends the Americans murdered one of my best men while he simply walked down the street in Berlin, minding his own business."

Alexi's surprised reaction was exactly what Pushkin was hoping for.

"What, you didn't think the wonderful Americans were capable of brutality?" Laughing derisively, he said, "You naïve fools."

Releasing Alexi's hair, Pushkin again approached Tamara, where he gently caressed her face before he suddenly and violently used both hands to tear her shirt from her body, causing her to shudder in fear and Alexi to painfully turn his head to see both his wife and her oppressor. His gaze intent on Alexi, Pushkin slipped the brassiere from Tamara's breasts as he gently caressed and cupped one breast with his right hand.

"Perhaps if you tell me the name of your handler and how to contact him, it won't go so badly for your wife."

His eyes never left Alexi's as he slowly squeezed Tamara's breast in a vice-like grip until she could stand the pain no longer and cried out.

"STOP!" Alexi finally screamed.

Pushkin momentarily loosened his grip while the hand remained in place.

"Are you ready to cooperate?"

"If you let her go, yes."

Reaching behind him, Pushkin removed a knife from the small of his back and in quick successive moves cut the ties which bound Tamara to her chair. She instantly rushed to her husband and kneeled to embrace him. Shoving her out of the way, Pushkin told Alexi, "Give the information to

Captain Ovechkin," as he moved to the table and again inspected the confiscated gear.

Captain Ovechkin, who until now had remained motionless and out of the way, quickly stepped forward, a notepad and pen having materialized in his hands. He kneeled in front of Alexi, as if in supplication, and wrote as Alexi slowly and quietly spoke. The one-sided conversation completed, Ovechkin rose and approached his superior officer, handing him the notepad.

Reading, Pushkin looked at his comrade and said, "As I suspected, this is one of Colonel Castle's men."

Quickly walking to Tamara, who was standing to the side, as if lost, Pushkin withdrew his pistol from its holster and swiftly shot her in the head. Turning back to Alexi, he did the same, just as Alexi was turning his head and opening his mouth in anguished protest.

Returning the gun to its resting place, Pushkin walked to Ovechkin and said, "Polozhi Troopi shto Amerikansi vyeedzeelyi ee znalye shto eto zameestseet za Vasily. (Put the bodies where the Americans are sure to find them and make sure they know this is payback for Vasily.)"

Pocketing the notepad, the Colonel exited the room, not bothering to close the door behind him.

PACIFIC NORTWEST, UNITED STATES
1983

On a secluded two lane road winding its way through a heavily forested area of the Umpqua National Forest, deep within the Cascade Mountain Range, a late model Ford Galaxy was speeding over the wet asphalt. Sheets of rain, combined with a total lack of moonlight, made for a treacherous driving experience. Headlights were reflected off the wet street and falling rain. Yet, James Wilson kept his foot firmly planted on the accelerator, causing his wife, Linda, to grasp whatever handhold made itself available. Glancing into the back seat to make sure that Steven, their three-year-old son, was firmly strapped into his new car seat, she turned back to look out the windshield, which was streaked and smeared by the swiftly moving wipers.

"Jimmy, please slow down. You can't even see where we're going."

Not taking his eyes from what little could be seen of the road, he replied, "I want to get as far away as we possibly can, as quickly as we can."

Motioning to their son, who was, somehow, still sleeping, she said, "I agree. But I'd like to do it in one piece."

Reluctantly, James eased off of the accelerator, immediately causing the car to slow to a somewhat more reasonable, if not quite safe, speed.

"I still can't believe how much we've been lied to. Those bastards!" For emphasis, he pounded the steering wheel, which caused the car to veer slightly and elicited a sleeping squeal from the back seat.

Reaching out for James' arm, Linda gently caressed it in an effort to calm her distraught husband. "I know, sweetheart. But we're away now and they'll never find us. We have everything we need to hunker down and raise our son."

Using the rear-view mirror to glance at his sleeping son, James took a deep, calming breath, which worked, at least in the short-term. "I know, but I'll still feel better the further we get."

His attention back to the road, he peered through the smeared windshield as he gently pressed the accelerator down to gain speed, hoping that his wife didn't notice. The fact they hadn't seen another car in hours gave him confidence in both their escape plan and his driving through these hazardous conditions. Unexpectedly, the rain suddenly intensified, as if being applied by a firehose.

Frightened, Linda grasped her handhold even tighter and said, "Maybe we should look for a place to pull over and wait this out."

Following a loud crack of thunder, Steven, stirring from his slumber, suddenly cried out, "Momma!"

As Linda turned to comfort her son with her one free hand, James said, "You know, pulling over somewhere doesn't seem like such a bad idea."

Relieved, she loosened her death grip and said, "Thank you."

Slowing to search for a safe haven, they entered a sharp curve, which was abruptly lit by a flash of lightning, which revealed a car headed straight at them, headlights off. Wrenching the steering wheel hard to the right, the other car performed the opposite maneuver, just a moment too late, and clipped the rear of James's vehicle, sending it careening down a steep ravine. The trees into which it crashed put a stop to both the car and the screams which had filled it on the way to its inevitable end. On the road, the other car's brake lights momentarily lit the area just before it sped away. Ten minutes later, the rain had slowed enough to allow for a safer driving experience. Traveling in the same direction in which James and Linda had been driving, a pair of headlights slowly entered the last curve James and Linda would ever experience. Noticing the damage to the foliage adjacent to the road, the driver slowed to a crawl as he peered into the gloom. Seeing a small fire, he immediately pulled over to assess the situation.

RENAISSANCE BALTIMORE HARBORPLACE HOTEL
BALTIMORE, MARYLAND, USA
OCTOBER, 2010

Seated at a table with my girlfriend, Lisa Jones, I couldn't help but comment. "You know, this is rather cheesy."

Our companions looked up from their drinks and conversations to take in our surroundings. Our companions this evening were Leonard Williams, twenty-eight, medium height and dark hair, wearing fashionable eye glasses and clothing, his brother Gerald Williams, twenty-nine, also of medium height with dark hair, but carrying himself with infinitely more confidence than his sibling, and Jennifer Turner, twenty-nine, a beautiful tall brunette with high cheekbones and a thin nose. I am Stephan Beck, the old-man of the group at thirty. Lisa is twenty-eight, short with dark hair and, to me, extremely attractive, although I've heard others describe her as average. Except for me, everybody at my table were graduates of the Franklin Private School System. Lisa had asked me to accompany her, and I gladly accepted, which explained why I found myself at a reunion of a school I had not attended.

On stage, a band was playing cover songs from the 80s and 90s while a spinning disco ball reflected fractured light throughout the room. Affixed to the wall behind the band was an enormous banner which read, "Welcome Graduates of the Franklin Private School System 1990 -1999." A bar was open along the back wall. On the dance floor, men and woman were dancing, while around them others were sitting at tables or milling about.

"OK, I'll give you cheesy, but in a classy sort of way," observed Gerald.

"The only thing even remotely classy about this affair is this hotel," opined Jennifer.

"Although," Lisa chimed in, "the 90s were kind of cheesy, as well, so this is pretty accurate."

Laughing, we all clinked glasses by way of acknowledgment.

Leonard, characteristically, was quietly scanning the room. He turned back to the group and said, "It's amazing how many people who went to school at Franklin's wound up getting together as couples."

At this, they all scanned the room. Since I hadn't gone to the school, I could not make an assessment, accurate or otherwise.

"You know, Len, I believe you are correct." Continuing her scan, Jennifer continued, "it's actually kind of weird."

"And creepy," contributed Gerald. Turning to Lisa and me, he noted, "You two seem to be the aberration."

Lisa agreed. "I never really noticed it, but it's as if Franklin's was a combination school and dating service."

"Now that would be great marketing!" said Gerald.

Jennifer turned to Len and asked, "So, find anything to your liking?"

Leonard's response, "That's usually not the issue," surprised me, even if it belied his lack of confidence.

"I keep telling you, bro, sitting on the sidelines is not going to get it done. You have to play the game to have any chance of winning," advised his brother.

"I'm working on it," was Leonard's response.

Turning to me in what I suspect was an effort to deflect the unwanted attention directed at him, Leonard said, "You're quiet this evening."

Shrugging, I told him, "It's not my reunion and I don't know most of these people, so I'm in more of a recon mode." Having said that, I looked around the room and noted, "Although, for some reason, a lot of these people look slightly familiar."

In response, Gerald quipped, "After a while, all of us Franklin graduates begin to look alike."

"Especially as we age," Jennifer observed.

To Lisa and Jennifer, Gerald said, "Now there's a project for you two scientific geniuses to work on."

"What's that?" asked Lisa.

"Something to keep us all young and sharp," replied Gerald.

Turning to Lisa, Jennifer mockingly asked, "Has he been spying on us?"

"Sounds like it," said Lisa as she turned to Gerald. "I'm sorry, but now we're going to have to kill you."

Gerald held his hands up in surrender as the music stopped and the lights dimmed and returned and dimmed and returned once again, getting everybody's attention. On stage, Headmaster Garrick Payne, a tall, distinguished looking, well-dressed man in his late 60s, with graying hair, stood at the microphone patiently waiting for the crowd to notice him and become quiet. Leaning into the microphone in front of him, he gently cleared his throat, the sound carrying through the speaker system. Quickly, the room quieted, as the attention of the occupants was drawn to the stage, where a live image of the Headmaster was showing on a screen which had been lowered from the ceiling behind him.

I could see Lisa searching her immediate surroundings, looking for something and not finding it. Leaning over, she whispered to me, "Stephan, I don't have my phone. Would you record this for me, please?"

Nodding, I reached into my pocket, pulled out my phone, and began recording the Headmaster's speech, just as *La Voltaire et La Franklein* began to play in the background.

"Thank you everybody. I'm Headmaster Payne and I'd like to welcome you all and thank you for joining us tonight, as well as for your continued support of our programs. As you can readily ascertain, you and your classmates, our graduates, are immensely successful in all walks of life. Our goals have been, and continue to be, to activate your search for knowledge, activate your ability to learn, and activate your desire to achieve your goals. You contribute to society at the highest levels of politics, science, medicine, the military, and nearly every other avenue of import. I want to personally thank you for your continued efforts and look forward to utilizing our methods of teaching with your children so that we, as a community, may continue to contribute well into the future. So, please, give yourselves a round of applause and enjoy the remainder of the evening."

As his speech concluded, the music once again began as the room burst into applause. He took all of this to be directed at him and stood basking in the adoration, his visage remaining on the screen behind him as he waved to the crowd. Everybody's rapt attention was focused on the screen and the music, so I panned the room with my camera phone to capture the experience for Lisa. As the music faded and the Headmaster left the stage, the lights became less dim and the room became oddly quiet, as if its occupants were waking from a dream.

UNITED GENETICS RESEARCH LAB
JANUARY, 2011

The main conference room was a masterful bit of interior design: tasteful and elegant, yet not opulent. The distinction was important, especially when presenting to potential investors who want to know their money is being applied to scientific advancement and not artistic extravagance.

On this day, Lisa Jones and Jennifer Turner, clad in white lab coats over their regular street clothes, were joined by two similarly dressed colleagues on one side of the oval glass and mahogany table. Opposite them sat three representatives of potential investment firms: Robin Gage, forty-six years old and impeccably dressed in Dior, representing her family's investment fund, Gage Investments; Arthur Williams, fifty-six years old and conservatively dressed in a gray pin-striped suit, representing People for Scientific Advancement, a private equity fund; and Edward Effingham, sixty-two years old and dressed casually in pressed jeans and a button-down shirt, representing The Effingham Group, an investment firm started by his immigrant father in the early 1990s. At the head of the table stood the Chief Operating Officer of United Genetics Research Lab, Dr. Howard Schwartz, sixty years old, dressed in a conservative blue business suit.

"So, in conclusion, I would like to stress that what we are attempting to do here in targeting specific genetic markers for specific diseases, will change the way that disease is treated in the future, as well as possibly allowing for the eradication of certain genetically transmitted diseases. Now, to today's reality. The type of work that we do, and which we propose to do in the future, requires funds. As a private company, we have made the philosophical decision to utilize only private funds. We do not want to be burdened with the strings that accompany governmental money, nor the likely distortion of our research, as is so often the case when dealing with the government. Hopefully, you agree with both our goals and our philosophy and will recommend to your funds that they invest in our work and the future of modern medicine. Thank you for your time."

Instead of retaking his seat, Dr. Schwartz moved to the side of the table which housed the potential investors and approached each with an outstretched hand. Jennifer, Lisa, and their colleagues, taking their cue from the boss, did the same. Soon, all participants were milling about, exchanging pleasantries and assuring one another that the presentation had gone well.

Ms. Cage and Mr. Williams, having left the conference room, Ed Effingham lagged behind, and, as the last of the investor group remaining in the room, approached Dr. Schwartz, extended his hand and said, "Dr., I am very impressed with your work here at the Lab. It has deep personal meaning to me, my father having died from cystic fibrosis. As I am the final decision maker at my firm, I can assure you we will be investing in your work." He reached into his pocket, removed a business card, and handed it to the astounded Dr. Schwartz. "Please have your lawyers contact me so that we can get the necessary paperwork started."

Dr. Schwartz accepted the card and stared at it, as if he had never seen such an object before. He gathered himself and replied, "Thank you very much, Mr. Effingham. We appreciate your confidence."

"It's my pleasure. I'm pleased to have the ability to contribute personally towards improving the world."

•　　•　　•

Two weeks later, an amazingly short period of time for such a monumental transaction to have been completed, Jennifer and Lisa sat across from Dr. Schwartz's desk. All dressed in casual clothing, with Jennifer and Lisa both sporting open white lab frocks over their street clothes. Dr. Schwartz looked immensely pleased, like the proverbial cat which ate the canary.

"Howard, you look extremely pleased with yourself," noted Jennifer.

Looking at Jennifer, Lisa remarked, "He does, doesn't he?" Focusing her attention back on her boss, she said, "So, how long are you going to make us wait for whatever news we know you're just dying to tell us?"

Responding with a silent grin that spread from ear to ear, he continued to look from one to the other until, finally, he laughed and said, "OK. I've tortured you enough. The Effingham Group has come through and provided enough funding for us to move full steam ahead on the targeted genetics research." Satisfied, he leaned back in his chair and waited for the reaction from his two leading researchers, both of whom sat straighter in their chairs, looked at one another as each sported a grin to match their bosses, and then refocused on Dr. Schwartz.

"That's amazing," gushed Lisa.

"I can't believe how quickly that happened," added Jennifer.

"The fact of the grant and the speed with which it occurred are both amazing," responded Dr. Schwartz. Gazing at the women, he gathered they had not yet fully grasped the reason for having them in his office. Leaning forward and placing his elbows on the desk, he asked, "You know what this means, right?"

A little puzzled, Jennifer and Lisa looked at one another before Lisa responded with a tentative, "That we get to keep our jobs?"

Chuckling, Dr. Schwartz said, "Of course, that. As a matter of fact, an expansion of that. You will both head up your own teams and get your own labs."

Once again looking at one another as they took in the news, each sported a grin that threatened to fracture their faces. Spontaneously, they high-fived each other.

Pleased, Dr. Schwartz continued, "Congratulations. You both deserve this. You've been doing great work together. I imagine that a little friendly competition will spur you on to even greater things."

Simultaneously, they responded, "Thank you!"

"You're welcome. Now, both of you get out of my hair. We all have a lot of planning to do, and by all, I mean the two of you."

They arose from their chairs as if one, and again both said, "Thank you," as they headed for the room's exit, the way illuminated by the bright glow which emanated from their beings.

UNITED STATES ARMY INTELLIGENCE AND SECURITY COMMAND (INSCOM) HEADQUARTERS
FORT BELVOIR, VIRGINIA

I worked at INSCOM, an enormous facility which housed over fifty thousand employees, both military personnel and civilian contractors. My job was to interpret intercepted messages which were spoken in Russian, in which I was, and remain, fluent. I've always had an affinity for languages, although I can't say from where that affinity originated. My parents, who were both fluent in only their native English (the American variety) always said I was gifted by the language gods as I not only spoke Russian, but could get by in both Spanish and Italian, as well as various other Slavic based languages.

Although the base was huge, I rarely had the luxury of working in a private office, those being reserved for personnel of higher rank. I was a Sergeant and, while it's better than being a Private, it didn't afford me the privileges of higher rank. However, on this day I was able to snag an office, most people being at a training session. Taking full advantage of this rare opportunity, the door was closed, headphones clamped tightly over my ears and my eyes firmly closed as I concentrated on the words being fed into my ears. Unexpectedly, something clasped my shoulder, which startled me so much that my butt slid perilously from the cushion and the headphones were yanked from their preferred cranial location, strange sounding roughly spoken Russian seeping from the ear holes and escaping into the air as they made their way to the floor. As my eyes flew open, I focused on Sergeant Major Cade Williams standing before the desk, a bemused yet somehow still annoyed look etched on his face. I regained my composure and stood to salute when he motioned for me to stay in my seat, or at least retake it, which I gladly did.

"How's the translation coming, Beck?"

"Ya Nye Slishil. Shot Vhi Zashlee. (Sorry, sir. I didn't hear you come in)."

"You're speaking Russian."

"Sorry sir. My brain hasn't made the transition yet."

Waiting for an answer to his previous question, and receiving none as my mind slowly made its way back to English, Sergeant Major Williams had to repeat himself, which he rarely appreciated, this being no exception to the rule.

"How's the translation coming?" he asked, a hint of annoyance coloring the tone of his voice.

I shook my head to clear it as I replied, "It's coming, but slowly. There's a lot of interference and it sounds somewhat mechanical. It's also a dialect you don't hear much, but I'll get it, sir."

"I'm sure you will, Beck. That's why we gave it to you."

"Thank you, sir. I won't let you down."

"I'm sure you won't. Get back to it. The brass is eager to hear what you have to say about this."

I replied, "Yes sir," to his retreating back and the closing door. I bent to retrieve the headphones when the desk phone rang and the light on the phone blinked, once again startling me. My concentration now completely shot, I reached for the phone and lifted the handset.

"Beck here."

The responding voice brought a smile to my entire face.

"Hi hon. What's up?"

In response, Lisa reminded me of our dinner at her parent's house and let me know she was running a little late.

"No problem. I'll work a little later and meet you there. See you soon. Love you."

I returned the handset to its cradle, replaced the headphones in their proper place, rewound the tape, and, before too long, was once again "in the zone."

• • •

Just after 7:00 pm I was standing on the portico of a modest, but well-kept Georgian style house. I rang the dimly lit bell and almost immediately the door opened and a beaming Lisa warmly greeted me, as if she had been waiting with her hand on the doorknob.

"Hey there, handsome," was how I was received.

"Hey there, to you," I responded as I moved in for a kiss, which I gladly received. Stepping back, I said, "You look wonderful, as always."

"Flattery will get you whatever you want, babe."

I reached for her as she laughed and backed out of the way, making room for me to pass through the now wide-open door. I obliged and said, "Teaser," as I passed her and entered the foyer on my way to the kitchen, followed closely by Lisa.

"Are you limping?" she asked.

Unconsciously, I rubbed my leg and said, "Is it noticeable?"

"It is."

I stopped and turned to face her. "My leg is bothering me a little today. It's been a long day."

She placed her hand on my arm and, with genuine concern, said, "We need to get that looked at."

"I know. I will."

"You keep saying that."

Trying to keep annoyance from seeping into my voice, I said, "I know. And I mean it. As soon as I can find the time."

I think my attempt at removing any hint of annoyance was only partially successful, as she backed off and said, "OK."

I knew when to let it go, and did so, turning to enter the kitchen where I saw Lisa's mother, Roxanne, placing the finishing touches on her signature salad. As we entered, Roxanne turned and, seeing us together, greeted me with a broad smile. She placed the knife on the counter and approached me on the other side of the kitchen island, where we exchanged European style air kisses to the space next to each cheek.

Handing her the bottle of wine I'd been cradling, I said, "Hi Mrs. J. How are you?"

Accepting the proffered gift, she replied, "I've been just fine, Stephan. It's so nice to see you. It seems as if it's been ages."

Rolling her eyes at the subtle dig, Lisa admonished, "Come on, Mom. You know how busy we've been. Don't start with the guilt trip."

Surrendering, Roxanne retreated to place the wine in the refrigerator as she replied, "OK, OK. You know, I just had to say *something*."

"I know how hard it is to control yourself," Lisa good-naturedly replied.

At that moment, I heard the sliding glass door open and saw Lisa's father, Peter, enter from the patio. Seeing me, he smiled and approached, holding his hand out in greeting, which I readily accepted.

"Hello Mr. Jones. Nice to see you. How've you been?"

"I'm well, Stephan, although I'll be better when you start calling me Peter."

I chuckled to myself as I responded, "I keep meaning to. It's just this military training kicking in. It's hard to let that go without thinking about it."

"You can work on it while you give me a hand outside. First, let me get us a couple of beers."

After having retrieved a beer for each of us, he led the way out to the patio, expecting me to follow, which I did. As I turned to close the sliding door, I glanced at Lisa, who gave me the thumbs-up sign just before she turned back to help her mother.

•   •   •

Lisa's parents had an affinity for tiki lights, so had surrounded the patio with them. While not a huge fan myself, I had to admit they lent a certain festive atmosphere to a gathering. Maybe I was becoming a tiki light convert.

It was in this lit atmosphere that Lisa and I found ourselves sitting with Leonard and Gerald Williams, Lisa's old schoolmates. Their parents, Greg and Susan, were old friends of the Joneses and were also present. Neither Lisa nor I had seen Leonard or Gerald since the reunion. In an effort to catch up, we discussed work, mostly, and it was in this vein that Lisa mentioned the happenings at the lab, including the fact that both Lisa and Jennifer were getting their own labs. At the mention of Jennifer, Leonard perked up. Had he been a puppy, his ears would have stood at attention and his butt done the doggy butt wiggle.

"So," Leonard tentatively began, "you and Jennifer will be in competition with one another."

"No, not really," Lisa mildly protested. After a brief pause for some reflection on the matter, she continued, "although, since we'll be working on the same project, I suppose we'll each want to get to the goal line first."

"So, you *will* be in competition. This could be very interesting."

"*Fine*, I suppose so," Lisa reluctantly agreed. "But a *friendly* competition."

"If you say so," a smiling Leonard retorted.

I noticed Leonard was becoming fidgety, as if something were on his mind and he couldn't decide whether to bring it up. "Come on, Len. There's obviously something on your mind. Spit it out," I prodded.

He looked at me with a look that said *"Really?"*, but instead said aloud, "Well, I was just wondering how Jennifer was doing."

At hearing that, Gerald sat up straight and paid rapt attention. "Wait, are you thinking about asking Jennifer out?" asked his brother, unable to keep the incredulity from his voice.

Leonard glared at Gerald and responded as if he had been challenged. "Yes, I have been thinking about it. What of it?"

Cutting Gerald off before he could begin a brotherly row, Lisa said, "Do it."

This response helped to refocus Leonard, as he turned to Lisa and said, "Really? Do you know something? Has she said anything about me?"

Unable to resist, Gerald said, "What is this, seventh grade?"

Ignoring Gerald, Lisa said, "No, I don't know anything specific. I do know that she'd like to be in a relationship and she's comfortable with you."

Wanting both to encourage Leonard and stop Gerald from saying something infuriating, I said, "Do it. What do you have to lose?"

Suddenly, Leonard's mother, from the other side of the table, said, "Did I just hear that you're going to ask somebody on a date?"

"It's amazing how you can hone in on a conversation that has nothing to do with you, mother," replied Leonard. "And yes, I am going to ask somebody on a date."

In defense of herself, Susan said, "It's not as if you're in another room. You're sitting right here. I couldn't help but hear."

"Of course," was Leonard's only response. Directing his attention back to his peers, Leonard suggested we go inside for dessert.

"Good idea," responded Gerald in a surprising show of brotherly support.

As the four of us got up and headed for the sliding glass doors leading into the house, I stepped aside to allow the others to enter. Waiting, I glanced back to the table and saw Greg looking at me before leaning over to his wife's ear and whispering. As I turned to go through the door, I noticed Susan peering at me and shrugging non-committedly in response to whatever her husband had murmured. Wondering if I was just being paranoid, I entered the house and rejoined our friends.

UNITED GENETICS RESEARCH LAB
AND VARIOUS OTHER LOCATIONS
MARCH, 2011

Finally ensconced in their new offices, Lisa and Jennifer were each seated at their respective desks while they worked through a small portion of what seemed to be never ending paperwork. Each had boxes stacked on their floor, waiting to be unpacked. Both had identical lab setups: an office with a glass wall which looked out at a large lab space containing plenty of room for assistants and all the modern equipment each could possibly have hoped for, since each had provided a list of requested equipment. Although still interviewing research assistants, each had two hard at work.

Throughout the country, graduates of the Franklin School were also hard at work in their various vocations: scientists, doctors, lawyers, politicians, military personnel and other assorted jobs, doing Headmaster Garrick Payne proud.

At precisely 11:00 a.m., Eastern time, the telephones of a select group of these graduates, all of whom had been present at the reunion, rang, and were answered in turn. Each, including Lisa and Jennifer, heard a strange voice say "Hello," before the sounds of *La Voltaire et La Franklein* were fed through their ears and into their brains. Each of the listeners became glassy eyed, as if in a trance, before hearing a mechanically altered voice who recited a string of unrelated words and numbers spoken in Russian. Not everybody received the same message, each having been tailored for the individual recipient, but each heard the same supposedly male sounding mechanical voice. Abruptly, the call was ended by the instigator and each person having received the call slowly emerged from his or her trancelike state, surprised to see a telephone in his or her hand. Feeling strange, each replaced the telephone in the location from which it had been prior to the call and continued with whatever task they were performing before the strange event took place.

INSCOM HEADQUARTERS
ONE WEEK LATER

I was back at work, without the benefit of having a private office this time. Back to normal. Consequently, I sat at a slightly oversized cubicle among a throng of other slightly oversized cubicles. The larger size and curved walls provided a sense of privacy, false or otherwise. It was hard to tell, but I believe most of the other cubicles were also occupied by people doing the same or similar job as me. Since our job was to listen, not speak, even if filled to capacity, the room remained eerily quiet.

I had headphones clamped over my ears as I listened to a recording. The screen in front of me enabled me to manage various components of my auditory perception, with the goal of ensuring clear reception and comprehension of the intercepted information. It also displayed the source of the recording, in this case Homeland Security, and the date on which it had been recorded.

As I concentrated on my translation, a cacophony of noise suddenly bombarded my ears so loudly I involuntarily yelled, "Shit!" as I pulled the headphones off.

As I tried to re-situate myself, a head appeared over the rim of my cubicle and the smirking face of Corporal Joel Clark appeared.

"So, the Russian finally got to you. It was bound to happen."

Still hearing ringing in my ears, I could only mutter, "Funny. All of a sudden there was a loud noise that almost blew out my eardrums."

"That's how I feel whenever I hear Russian being spoken," he responded with a chuckle.

Having recovered enough to be more myself, I smiled at him and said, "Yeah, that Arabic you listen to is so sweet and soothing."

"Ha! We both picked some beautiful and romantic languages, didn't we?"

"I don't know if I chose it so much as it chose me," I said. Picking up my headphones, I continued, "At least I know what to look out for now. Back to work."

"Yes, sir," Corporal Clark responded as his head disappeared and we each returned to our assignments.

•   •   •

A few hours later, I was standing in front of my Commanding Officer's desk as he finished reviewing my report. Still reading, he motioned for me to have a seat, which I gladly did. At last, he looked away from the report and focused his attention on me.

"Are you certain this was an encrypted transmission and not just interference? Some of the stuff they send over is not of the best quality, which is why I think they send it to us in the first place."

"Yes sir. I agree that the quality of some of Homeland's recordings are not the best, but this has a different feel to it. It's not anything I can put my finger on just yet, but I think it's being masked to look like typical interference."

Looking skeptical, he asked, "Just a feeling on your part, huh?"

"Yes, sir. There's just something too regular or calculated in the irregularities, if you know what I mean."

"Honestly, I don't think I do." He glanced back at my report, obviously considering his response. Looking back at me, he said, "OK. I don't think Homeland thought we'd be able to do anything with it anyway, so I won't kick it back to them just yet. My contact tells me that, with this election coming up, they're worried about future funding, so, if you can find something useful, it will help to bolster their position. Take a crack at it, but don't spend all of your time on it. There's plenty of good quality stuff for you to listen to. It's not like the Russians went silent after the Cold War ended, and we have our own funding to worry about."

Relieved, I said, "Understood. Thank you, sir."

In response, he nodded and began shuffling papers on his desk. Understanding that I'd been dismissed, I stood, saluted, and made my escape.

UNITED GENETICS RESEARCH LAB

As the clock approached 5:00 p.m., Lisa's cell phone alarm went off, emitting the tones of *La Voltaire et La Franklein*. As she heard the music play, her eyes momentarily lost focus as her hand, of its own volition, reached to silence the alarm. She seemed puzzled by the fact that the song was her alarm, as she had no memory of downloading it or setting it as such. Regaining her poise, she looked through the window/wall of her office and saw her two assistants still hard at work. Smiling to herself at their dedication, she rose from her desk and moved to the door. To be better heard, she opened the door and stuck her head into the lab.

"Hey guys. You've both been putting in long hours. Call it a night and I'll see you in the morning."

Pleasantly surprised, they each looked up. The first said, "You're the boss!"

The other chimed in, "And who are we to argue with the boss?"

Laughing, Lisa said, "Exactly! Now, get out of here and go have some fun!"

Completing the tasks at which they had been working, the first replied, "Don't have to tell us twice!"

In unison, they said, "See you tomorrow," before heading out.

Alone, she reentered her office and stopped. Surveying the room, she seemed temporarily lost, as if she were an elderly person, having forgotten why she entered the room. Then an epiphany struck. She strode to the other end of the office, took a set of keys from her pocket and unlocked the waiting file cabinet. With renewed purpose, she rifled through the files until she located the desired one, quickly removed it, closed, and relocked the cabinet. File in hand, she turned and went into the empty lab. She placed the file on a counter, checked the contents, and began mixing chemicals. She used the equipment she had requested and checked the computer readouts. Now, totally in her own headspace, her concentration laser focused, she experimented with various combinations of chemicals and other compounds, making notations as she proceeded and placed them into the waiting file.

Time had no meaning.

•   •   •

Elsewhere in the building, Jennifer was at her desk concentrating on deciphering some mathematical equation when she heard a quiet knock on her open office door. Looking up, she saw Leonard framed in the doorway, sheepishly holding a bouquet of flowers. The sight brought a smile to her face as she came around the desk to greet him. Before she could take her third step, her cell phone alarm went off, emitting the tones of *La Voltaire et La Franklein*. As the composition played, a lost, unfocused look found its way onto both of their faces. Moving to turn the alarm off, both were momentarily frozen in place until, simultaneously, they shook it off and continued with their previous objective.

Accepting the flowers from his outstretched hand, she kissed him on the cheek and said, "Thank you, Len. That's sweet."

"That's me. Thoughtful and sweet."

As Jennifer headed into the lab to grab a beaker in substitution of a vase, he asked, "About ready to go to dinner?"

Hesitating before answering, she finally said, "Would you mind if we had a late dinner? There's something I need to get started."

Having no other plans, Len said, "No problem. Mind if I hang out with you while I wait?"

Relieved, she responded, "That would be great."

Taking the beaker of flowers into her office, she found an empty spot on her desk and filled it with the beaker. She removed a set of keys from a desk drawer, unlocked a file cabinet, and removed a file. Waiving it at Leonard, she said, "To the lab."

She entered the lab, Leonard at her heels.

THE FRANKLIN SCHOOL
1988

In a small control room located adjacent to a larger classroom, behind a two-way mirror, Headmaster Payne stood motionless, staring into the classroom. He was accompanied by Yuri Ovechkin, dressed in casual civilian clothing meant to blend into the American style scene.

Only two individuals, Theresa Cook, a teacher in her mid-thirties, and six-year-old Lisa Jones occupied the classroom. Ms. Cook and Lisa faced each other, with Lisa sitting on a child-sized seat and Ms. Cook sitting on an adult-sized chair. The teacher leaned forward and lowered her face to better connect with her student on a personal level.

As they observed, Headmaster Payne told Mr. Ovechkin, "This one shows real promise. She comes under control easily. But...", his voice trailed off.

"But, what?"

"She shows a tendency to fight it off after initially succumbing to the treatment."

Ovechkin turned to face the Headmaster as he said, "And what are you doing about that?"

"We're working on it. She's only six-years-old. We're certain we'll be able to get it under control."

Returning to his observation, Ovechkin asked, "What is her name?"

"Lisa. Lisa Jones."

Searching his memory banks, Ovechkin said, "The child of Peter and Roxanne, from the first wave."

Impressed by his recall, the Headmaster replied simply, "Yes."

As Ovechkin watched the teacher and pupil, he instructed the Headmaster to increase the volume of the speakers in the room so that he could better hear what was being said. The Headmaster dutifully obliged.

"Very good, Lisa!" the teacher exclaimed.

Pleased to hear praise being heaped upon her, Lisa beamed and waited expectantly for her next question or task. As she did so, Ms. Cook turned to the desk, opened a drawer, and removed a syringe which had been pre-loaded with an opaque yellow liquid. Instantly, the look on Lisa's face changed to one trying to mask horror, and failing.

"I know you don't like needles, Lisa, but it's time for your vitamins. You want to grow up healthy and strong, don't you?" she asked rhetorically.

Gulping, Lisa looked at the floor and quietly replied, "Yes, Ms. Cook," even though no answer had been required or expected.

"Good! Now, let's get this done quickly so we can continue your lessons."

Without further warning, Ms. Cook leaned over, swabbed Lisa's arm with alcohol, and expertly administered the shot.

"There, that wasn't so bad, was it?"

Now having a hard time keeping her eyes opened, Lisa said, "No, Ms. Cook," as her head became too heavy for her neck and her chin rested on her chest.

Taking Lisa's face in one hand and using her other to lift the eyelids and do a cursory examination, she let the chin fall, turned to the mirror and nodded, not expecting, nor receiving, a response. Turning back to Lisa, her demeanor transformed from that of a kindly school teacher to a determined researcher in the middle of a delicate experiment while being watched by her superiors.

Clapping her hands together loudly in front of Lisa's sleeping face, she sternly said, "Leesa! Bistra Stavoy!" ("Lisa, wake up! Now!")

In response, Lisa slowly lifted her head and opened her eyes, looking directly at the pseudoscientist sitting before her.

"Preekrasno." ("Good.")

Reaching back to the desk, Ms. Cook pressed a hidden button. The lights dimmed and the room filled with seemingly random sounds: beeps, buzzes, hisses, and musical notes. Within minutes, Lisa was in a deep, trancelike state, staring intently at the person facing her. Ms. Cook scrutinized her charge and noted the condition of her subject. She once again pressed the button, bringing the room back to its normal state.

"Nacheenayim." ("Now, let's begin.")

LISA'S APARTMENT
2011

Stephan is driving through a raging thunderstorm. The car is not one he recognizes, but, nevertheless, he feels comfortable behind the wheel. For a reason he cannot understand, he is nervous and sweating profusely. He doesn't think it's because of the driving conditions, but perhaps it's adding to his anxiety. Visibility is poor as the wipers streak rapidly across the windshield, doing their best to keep up with the downpour. The road is winding, lined with trees, and unfamiliar to Stephan. Unable to make himself slow down, the car accelerates through curves, sliding and on the verge of being out of control. Loud, high pitched static is blaring from the radio, causing his head to throb. He glances at the radio, as if just noticing that nothing intelligible is coming from its speaker. Slapping at the dial, he manages to turn it off, causing his headache to subside. Immediately, a noise from the empty back seat draws his attention, prompting him to take his eyes off the road ahead. His attention is wrenched back to the front of the car as bright white lights appear. Stephan jerks the steering wheel to the right, causing the car to fishtail on the wet pavement and...

I woke with a start and abruptly sat up in bed just in time to see a flash of lightning illuminate the world outside the window, the curtains being of no use against the white hot electricity. I wiped the cold sweat from my forehead, not having realized that I had been sweating. All that movement must have woken Lisa, since she turned on her nightstand light and reached out to touch me as I sat there, unaware of my current surroundings. Her touch sent a shockwave through my body, inducing me to jump in place.

"Another nightmare?"

Unable to yet speak, I simply nodded as I got up and went to the window. Moving the curtain aside, I stared at the falling rain, jumping inside my skin each time another flash of lightning occurred. After a moment, I walked to the bathroom, doing my best to hide the hitch in my giddy-up, knowing my attempt to be unsuccessful. After dowsing my face with cold water, I dried and went back to bed, embarrassed as I got under the covers.

Concerned, Lisa said, "Are you ok?"

"Yeah, I'm fine. Just another bad dream. You'd think at my age thunderstorms wouldn't affect me like this," I said, dejectedly.

"Age has nothing to do with it," she replied as she gently stroked my arm. "I noticed your limp seemed to be more pronounced."

Unconsciously rubbing my leg, I said, "Yeah. You know it always gets worse during this kind of weather."

"I know." After a moment of silence, she asked, "Was it the same nightmare?"

"Basically, but something seemed different." I paused and thought about the experience from which I'd just awakened. Turning to look at Lisa, I said, "There was some sort of noise that I don't recall from other episodes. I can't quite put my finger on it."

"Hm. Noise. Can you remember where it was coming from?"

Concentrating, it finally came to me. "The radio! It was coming from the radio."

"Was it music, or a song?"

After a moment, I was able to recall the sound. "No, it was just noise, like loud static, but pulsing. And not rhythmically. More random. It caused my head to hurt."

"Sounds like the problem you had at work the other day with that recording."

I just stared at her before I exclaimed, "You're a genius! That's exactly what it was!"

She laughed as she said, "You don't need to be Freud to figure that one out."

"Maybe not," I said, "but you got there much faster than I did, Madam Sigmond."

She could see that I was feeling better and reached to turn the light off, saying, "Come back to bed."

"I'm too awake to sleep."

She reached over and pulled me down. "Then let's find a way to drain some of that energy."

I happily submitted to her therapy.

INSCOM HEADQUARTERS

I went back to work, more anxious than ever to get back to the mystery recording from Homeland Security. Even though I had been spending a good amount of time on it over the past few days, I had my orders to move on to some other matters. For some reason, the nightmare reignited my stubborn desire to figure it out.

I was feeling good when I started the morning. A cup of terrible commissary coffee accompanied me to my cubicle as I settled in, called the recording up on my computer and placed the headphones in their customary position. With my eyes closed in my usual concentration pose, I worked the computer controls in an effort to filter out whatever noise I felt needed to be removed. After listening and fiddling for hours, I removed the headphones and slammed my fist on the desk in frustration.

"Damn! Damn, damn, damn!"

Moments later, the face of Corporal Clark slowly appeared from the other side of our shared cubicle wall.

"Let me guess. It's not going well this morning."

Looking at him with the most sarcastic look I could muster, I said, "It's almost as if you can read minds."

"Yeah, I've been told that before. Plus, the shaking of my equipment as you assaulted your desk was a huge clue."

I laughed and said, "Sorry."

"No problem. You still working on that piece the Captain told you to let go?"

Looking around, I lowered my voice to a conspiratorial level as I said, "Quiet, and yes."

"Dude, give it up. You're making yourself crazy, and you're going to get caught. It's not worth it."

"I know. You're right. I just can't seem to let it go."

"You're starting to worry me. If you're going to insist on working on it, try to keep a lower profile. Beating up your desk is bound to get you noticed."

"You're right. I'll give it one more shot and then call it quits. Sorry if I screwed up anything you were working on."

"No problem. Glad you're going to see the light."

His face disappeared from view as I heard a noise and turned my head to look behind me. Unfortunately, I was also reaching for my coffee cup and, not having eyes in the back of my head, knocked it over, spilling the liquid everywhere, including my computer keyboard.

I hissed, "Shit!," as quietly as I could and reached for the box of tissues in an attempt to stem the tide of dark water cascading from the keyboard and desk. I wiped, mopped and blotted as best I could, causing havoc to my computer settings as I inadvertently hit dials, knobs, and switches. After completing my cleanup, I placed the headphones over my ears so that I could try to find the baseline I had just destroyed. Upon doing so, I immediately heard the hissing sound which had been driving me crazy. Reaching for a control, I was about to adjust it when I caught the faintest hint of a word, "Meeseeya (Mission)," escape between bursts of the noise which had been mocking me. Instantly, I hit pause and made a note of where in the recording the word had appeared. Thinking to myself, "*I knew it!*" I tried not to get overly excited, lest I give myself away to the room. Instead, I calmly plugged my phone into the computer and, against every regulation in the book, recorded the intercepted "message." My reasoning was that I could work on it outside of working hours, thereby keeping up with my workload and also abiding, in spirit, if not in actuality, with the orders handed down by my Captain.

It's amazing how easily one can rationalize breaking the law. I've discovered it's best not to dwell on it.

WASHINGTON, DC
2011
1789 RESTAURANT

The 1789 Restaurant was one of those old, established political haunts favored by the old, established politicians entrenched in and around Washington, D.C. The décor was dark wood, polished to a high gloss, and white linen tablecloths with gleaming silverware.

Three people were seated at a table in the middle of the restaurant, obviously having a working dinner, as evidenced by the small portfolio and notepad taking up the space where a fourth person would normally sit. The older gentleman at the table was Leonid Pushkin, now seventy-years-old. He was joined by Yuri Ovechkin, currently the Russian Ambassador to the United States, and Cheryl Rosen, a forty something year-old woman and a curator at the Smithsonian Institute.

At his most charming, Pushkin turned his attention to Ms. Rosen. "So, Ms. Rosen, Ambassador Ovechkin tells me you'd like to examine some of our little trinkets."

"Please, call me Cheryl, and yes, I'd love to examine what you refer to as your 'trinkets.' As head of the Russian History Section at the Smithsonian, I'm very interested to see what you'll be exhibiting. From what little I've been able to hear through the grapevine, there are items that haven't been displayed for decades."

Ambassador Ovechkin replied instead of his old boss. "Cheryl, if we can arrange it, and I want to repeat, *if*, it will have to wait until we get everything unpacked and have the exhibit set up. There is much work to do before that."

"Mr. Ambassador, it would be most helpful if we could have access prior to that. I'd like to proceed with a high level of detail and without a crowd."

Stepping in, Pushkin said, "Cheryl, I'm sure you would, but timing may be an issue. It will all depend on the arrangements that I am able to make. I will do my best to accommodate you and the Smithsonian. After all, we have been great friends over these last few years."

"Thank you, Mr. Pushkin. The end of the Cold War has done wonders for our relationship. I'm very much looking forward to having your cultural treasures shared with our citizens."

Raising their glasses, the three shared a friendly toast.

•　　•　　•

At the maître d stand, two men approached and spoke to the waiting attendant. Pushkin, hearing what he believed was a familiar voice, allowed himself an ironic inner smile. As the men approached on the way to their table, Pushkin rose and blocked the route, holding his hand out in greeting to his old nemesis, Dan Fowler, now a sixty-eight-year-old civilian.

"Hello, Dan. It's been a long time. I hope you and your loved ones are well."

Ignoring the proffered hand, Dan coldly replied, "Yes, it has been a long time."

Ambassador Ovechkin, having remained seated, rose and faced Dan and his companion, General William Eastsea.

"Hello Dan. Nice to see you." Turning his attention to the General, the Ambassador held his hand out in greeting and said, "Hello General. Nice to see you again."

General Eastsea graciously accepted the outstretched hand and replied, "Thank you, Mr. Ambassador. Nice to see you as well."

Pushkin, seeing that nobody had addressed the third party at their table, said, "How rude of me. Let me introduce you to Ms. Cheryl Rosen. She is head of the Russian History Section at the Smithsonian. We hope to continue our mutual cooperation regarding cultural matters with that esteemed institution. Cheryl, this is Dan Fowler and General Eastsea. The General sits on the Joint Chiefs of Staff."

"Nice to meet you both," said Cheryl. She remained seated, sensing an unspoken tension between her hosts and Dan Fowler.

For an awkward moment, the Russians and Fowler stared at each other in silence. Finally, Fowler said, "Well, isn't this civilized of us?"

"Yes, it is," answered Pushkin. "Not quite like the old days."

In response, Fowler made a point of looking Pushkin and Ovechkin up and down before he said, "You two seem to have done very well for yourselves. The fall of the Empire has worked out for the best."

"One does what one can under the circumstances with which one is presented," responded Pushkin.

"Yes, taking advantage of the circumstances was always a specialty of yours, wasn't it? What was it this time, oil?"

In response, Ovechkin said, "Oil, diamonds, what difference does it make? Despite what you would like to believe, we are a legitimate businessman and statesman. Your bitterness, or perhaps jealousy, is misplaced."

Clearly resentful, Fowler said, "Yes, a businessman and statesman. I'm certain it was all 'legitimate.' Enjoy your dinner. Nice to meet you, Miss Rosen." Not waiting for his companion, Fowler walked off to find his table with the ever patient maître d.

Shrugging, as if to inform the others that he was not responsible for his friend's behavior, General Eastsea said, "It was nice to see you all," as he followed in Fowler's wake.

The two standing Russians retook their seats as Cheryl said, "That Mr. Fowler seemed, how shall I say it...put off at seeing the both of you. How are you acquainted?"

Pushkin and Ovechkin glanced at one another, Ovechkin shrugging and nodding his head before Pushkin responded, "We used to be in the same business."

"Competitors, as it were," added Ovechkin.

"Really?," asked an intrigued Ms. Rosen. "And what business might that be?"

"We were spies, of course!" replied a jovial Pushkin.

Not knowing what to make of this statement, Cheryl nervously laughed and soon joined her companions in another toast. "To old spies!"

•   •   •

Seated at a booth along the wall and out of earshot of anybody else, Fowler and General Eastsea were sipping their drinks. Fowler was seething, the taste of his drink being lost in his anger.

"So, this is what it's come to. Those murdering bastards make billions of dollars and one of them actually becomes the Ambassador to the United States. And I have to be civil to them in a public restaurant in the United States of America. Un-fucking believable!"

"It's the brave new world we live in, Dan. New game, new rules. Things have changed since you and your Russian friends were running the show."

"Ha! Changed they have, and not for the better! Our politicians have really screwed this up." Fowler took a long drink before he continued his tirade. "We may have won the so-called Cold War, but it seems as if we're becoming more socialized and they're getting more capitalistic. What a colossal clusterfuck the whole thing turned out to be. And now we have the *War on Terrorism*. What bullshit."

In reply, General Eastsea said, "It's not as bad as all that. After all, the terrorism machine is keeping our funding way up. The shit we can do now is like science fiction compared to what you were doing back in the day."

"You're funding may be up now, but this election could change that. Have you heard what the Vice President had to say on that subject?"

Placing his drink on the table, the General answered, "I did, but it's just typical campaign bullshit. He knows he needs us, and to keep us working at peak efficiency, we need money, and he knows that, too. We'll be fine."

In response, Fowler said, "That may be, but he's the front runner and I don't like that shit coming from somebody in his position. It's just one more indication that society is going in the wrong direction. I wish there was something we could do about that."

Nodding in assent, General Eastsea picked up his drink and held it up in a mock toast. "Amen to that." Fowler picked up his drink and returned the gesture.

•　　•　　•

Having had a bit too much to drink to make driving a safe choice, Dan Fowler flagged down a cab and entered the backseat. After telling the driver his destination, Fowler closed his eyes and reflected on the evening's conversation. In doing so, he was reminded of a childhood incident.

•　　•　　•

Eight-year-old Dan Fowler woke in the night, feeling parched and in desperate need of a drink of water. Originally headed for the bathroom, he heard voices coming from downstairs and, assuming the voices belonged to his parents, took a detour. As he quietly descended the staircase, the voices became clearer. He recognized the voices as his parents', but they were speaking in a tone he was not used to hearing. Being only eight, he couldn't quite express it, but an older version of himself would describe it as anguish. Instinct told him to remain as quiet as possible, so he crept to the bottom stair and sat silently still.

First, he heard his father. "The shit is going to hit the fan in the next few days." Failing to hold back tears, his father said, "I don't know what I'm going to do."

Young Dan had never heard his father either say the "s" word or cry. He couldn't begin to fathom what was happening.

Next, he heard his mother. "How can you be so sure something is going to happen, and so soon?"

"Someone from the bank let slip the Feds were snooping around. They were specifically looking at the accounts of Fowler and Freed."

Surprised, his mother asked, "So, if you haven't done anything, there won't be anything for them to find. Right?"

A moment elapsed before the elder Fowler replied. "That's just it, Diane. There is something going on. Has been going on."

"What? Tell me." Little Dan had never heard his mother speak to his father with that tone of voice, and he was beginning to feel scared.

"We, Pete and myself, have been embezzling from the banks for years," his father admitted.

Immediately, Dan heard the sound a hand makes when slapping a face and could only imagine what had happened.

"How could you!?!" His mother was irate, and Dan really had no idea why.

Crying, his father said, "It started innocently, but business didn't get better and it got out of hand." Pleadingly, he continued, "We really didn't mean for it to get this far."

"How much?"

"Millions," came the choked reply.

"Oh my God! What are we going to do?! You could go to jail."

All Dan could think was, "My father is going to jail?"

The elder Fowler told his wife, "We can't let that happen. I realize how badly I've fucked up, but I can't do that to you and Dan."

"Really? You should have thought about that before you started stealing."

A short period of silence followed, and Dan thought the discussion was over. He slowly began to rise from his position when he heard his father's voice once again.

"Listen, I have it on good authority that Pete is planning on running. To Rhodesia. There's no extradition and, with the money he can take with him, he can live like a king."

"What about Dorothy? Is she OK with this? And the kids. What about them?"

Sheepishly, he said, "I don't think he's planning on taking them."

"That bastard!"

Dan couldn't believe his ears. His mother had said the "b" word! This must really be bad.

"I agree, but it could be an opportunity for me. For us."

"How so?"

"Well, if he runs, he looks guilty as hell. I think I can arrange it to look like it was all him and that I was duped, too."

"Go on," his clearly intrigued wife said.

Buoyed by this response, he continued. "So, if I can make it look like he did it on his own, the Feds will pin the whole thing on him and I can avoid jail. We can keep the house and Dan can grow up with his father."

After a moment of silence, she said, "That's a pretty shitty thing to do to your best friend and business partner."

"It's a pretty shitty thing for him to run and leave me holding the bag. It seems that it's every man for himself at this point."

"You're right," she replied with more authority in her voice. "It's shitty on everybody's behalf, but you've got to do what's best for you and this family."

Relief evident in his voice, he said, "Thank you. I guess this is an instance where the end justifies the means."

The conversation clearly having been completed, Dan rose and silently retraced the steps to his room, the drink of water having been forgotten as he tried to understand what he'd just heard.

• • •

"Hey, mister. We're here."

Awakened from his reverie, Dan looked out the window to see his darkened house waiting. He reached into his pocket, removed his wallet, and handed the cabbie a twenty-dollar bill for a nine-dollar fare.

"Keep the change," Dan told the cabbie as he opened the door.

"Thanks, mister. Have a good night."

UNITED GENETICS RESEARCH LAB

Lisa was alone in her office, sitting at her desk, staring into space, a blank look in her eyes. She looked extremely tired, the dark circles under her eyes making it look as if she'd been in a fight and lost. She wasn't asleep, but not quite awake, either. Suddenly, her whole body shook, and she became more conscious of her surroundings and her state of mind.

"What the hell is wrong with me?" she said aloud.

She stood, stretched, and walked to a cabinet on which awaited a cold pitcher of water. Pouring herself a glass and drinking it without pause, she felt a little more like herself. Replacing the glass, she stretched again, beginning with her neck and working her way to her toes.

"That's better." Glancing at the clock, she noted the late hour and said, "I need to get home and get some rest."

Having decided, she headed back to her desk and, as she gathered her things, heard the tones of *La Voltaire et La Franklein* emanating from her phone. Puzzled, she thought, *"I did not set that alarm,"* and reached to turn off what had become an annoyance. Sitting heavily in her chair, she held her head in her hands as she tried to regain control of herself, coming to the realization that something was not quite right. As she rose, her desk phone rang. Staring uncomprehendingly at it, she said, "What the hell?" Over her lifetime, she had been trained to answer a ringing telephone, so her hands couldn't resist reaching for it.

"Hello?"

A soothing male voice answered her, although, based on the sound, it could be the voice of any gender being filtered through a machine. "Hello, Lisa. Everything is fine. Take deep breaths and count backwards from ten."

Still fighting to control herself, she asked, "Who is this?"

In ever more soothing tones, the voice responded, "Lisa, it's OK. Deep breaths as you count backwards from ten." This time, a string of seemingly random sounds: beeps, buzzes, hisses, and musical notes followed the words. Instantly, Lisa followed the given orders and, breathing deeply, recited numbers in reverse order, beginning with ten. As she said, "one", she had become completely relaxed.

"Very good, Lisa. I'm so proud of you. Your work has progressed wonderfully."

Trancelike, she responded, "Thank you."

"Now, Lisa, you need to go back to work. Tonight. You are so very close to achieving your goal and time is getting short. Do you understand?"

"Yes." She hesitated before adding, "But I'm so tired."

"I know Lisa. Once you complete your assignment, you'll be able to relax and get some much needed sleep. But for now, you need to get back to work. You can finish tonight. I have all the confidence in the world in your abilities. Do you understand?"

"Yes, I do."

"Wonderful. When I hang up, you're going to be fully awake and full of energy. You'll go into your lab and get back to work."

"Back to work," is what came from her mouth, as if not quite connected to her brain.

"Yes."

Without warning, the call was disconnected. Lisa looked at the handset in her hand and briefly wondered why it was there before she replaced it, stood, and entered her lab, somehow refreshed.

DAN FOWLER'S HOME

Surrounded by darkness and illuminated by the glow of the computer monitor, Dan Fowler was sitting at the desk in his home office. Trying to occupy both his mind and his time, he sat and stared at a blank page as the unwavering cursor glowered at him with infinite patience, urging him, daring him, to write something. He had toyed with writing his memoir for quite some time, having started and discarded numerous attempts. The incident at the 1789 Restaurant the other night had him once again thinking that now was the time. He'd never attempted anything like this in earnest, the prior efforts having begun and ended as more of an exercise in futility. This time felt different, although the blank page still seemed to taunt him.

"Damn it, just start writing and it will come," he said aloud, echoing advice given to him long ago by an old and long forgotten friend. His fingers were poised above the keyboard, ready to follow the advice, when his phone rang, destroying the moment. Glancing at caller ID, a smile found its way to his lips as he reached for the phone and connected the call.

"Well, if it isn't my old Sergeant. How are you, Bob?"

"I'm well, Dan. How are you?"

"I'm just peachy, Bob. Absafuckinglutely peachy."

"Ha! It sounds like it."

"Right. Truth be told, I'm starting to go nuts from boredom. So much so that I'm even contemplating writing my memoir."

"Oh my God, you really are getting desperate! It seems I've called at just the right time."

"Why is that?"

"Before I say anything, is this a clean line?"

"Bob, I'm retired, not incompetent," replied Dan, unable to keep the annoyance from his voice.

"Dan, if I thought you were incompetent, I wouldn't have made this call, but I had to ask. You know that."

"I do. Sorry." After a beat, Dan asked, "So, why is this call so timely?"

"I'm becoming a little concerned with the state of affairs in this country. I understand that you're feeling the same way."

Dan thought to himself, "*The grapevine in this town has a life of its own.*" To Bob he said, "I take it you've spoken to the General."

"I have. We had lunch, and he mentioned you ran into some old friends, which led to you discussing some misgivings about the current campaign, as well as the general direction the country is headed."

Not willing to contribute any information, just yet, Dan simply said, "Go on."

"Let's say that I share your concerns, as do others."

"I'm not surprised. So, what's on your mind?"

"I think it may be advantageous for us to meet in person. It might lead to a way to alleviate some of that boredom you're experiencing."

"Let me know when and where, and I'll be sure to clear my schedule."

Laughing, Bob replied, "Will do," and disconnected the call.

Still holding the phone in his hand, he thought, "*Interesting.*"

JENNIFER'S APARTMENT

At 2:00 a.m., the bedroom was dark and quiet, the only sounds being the light snoring emanating from both Leonard and Jennifer. Even though her phone had been silenced, the screen glowed as it erupted with the sound of an old style telephone ring, startling both Jennifer and Leonard to a semi-awake state. Jennifer reached for the phone and noticed that the caller ID information had been blocked.

Muttering, "What the fuck?" she answered the call, her curiosity getting the better of her.

"Hello?"

"Hello Jennifer," a possibly machine modified voice responded.

Jennifer's face showed anger, then concentration, and finally a mischievous grin as she listened to the mysterious caller while Leonard watched.

"Who are you, and how do I contact you?"

Listening to the response, Jennifer glanced at Leonard, who silently mouthed, "Who is it?"

Ignoring him, Jennifer continued to listen before she said, "If you won't tell me who you are or how to contact you, why the hell should I trust anything you have to say?"

After listening to the caller, she responded, "OK," before she disconnected the call and replaced the phone on her nightstand.

Leonard, clearly perturbed at not having received any information about what had just transpired, sat up and turned on his bedside light. "What the hell was that?"

Staring at her ceiling and not bothering to look at Leonard, she dreamily replied, "I'm not sure."

"What do you mean, you're not sure? You just had a conversation that, from this side of it, didn't make a lot of sense. What did they want?"

After having tried to ignore him, she turned to focus her attention on Leonard and said, "It was a 'he', I think. It sounded like he was using some kind of voice modification device."

Leonard, now both annoyed and angry, said, "What the fuck did 'he' want at this hour?"

Seeing that Leonard was visibly angry, Jennifer forced herself to remain calm and quietly said, "Do not use that tone of voice with me," as she coldly stared at him.

Cowed, Leonard quietly responded, "Sorry."

"Better." In her normal tone of voice, she said, "He told me that Lisa beat me to the answer of what we were searching for. She actually figured out how to target specific DNA to fight specific diseases. Damn! I wanted that!"

"I thought you two weren't in any competition."

"Don't be an idiot! Of course, we were competing. Do you have any idea what that would've done for my career? And to have gotten it before *perfect Lisa* would've made it even sweeter. Damn it!"

Silence filled the room as Jennifer became lost in thought and Leonard mentally licked his wounds. A few moments later, Jennifer turned to Leonard and, with a wry smile plastered on her face, said "Whoever was on the phone also said that there may be a way I can get a win out of this, after all."

"How?"

"I'm not certain, yet. The only thing I can think of is that a peer review committee needs to check and recheck her work before it can be formally announced. He said he'd be in touch and then disconnected."

Turning away from Leonard and pulling the covers up to her nose, she said, "Turn the light off. I think it's going to be a very busy next few days."

Obediently, the room was once again plunged into darkness as Leonard got under the covers and stared at the back of his girlfriend's head, confused.

LISA'S APARTMENT

After having taken a couple of days off to rest and recuperate, Lisa was feeling better, but still not quite herself. The dark circles around her eyes remained as she took a sip of wine from the glass on the coffee table before letting her head loll back and closing her eyes. She had turned her phone off, lowered the shades, and drawn the curtains, making her apartment feel somewhat cave-like, which suited her mood. Since returning from the lab, she had been dressed only in her robe and underwear. Not expecting anybody to show up at her apartment, it startled her to hear a knock at the front door. Approaching the door in stealth mode, so she could withdraw without answering if she felt the need, she ventured to the peephole and placed her eye in position. Through the viewfinder, she saw Stephan bouncing up and down while he waited. As soon as she opened the door, he bounded into the room, excitement evident in every movement.

"You're not going to believe this! I had a minor accident at work, nothing catastrophic, but still. Anyway, that's not the part you won't believe. So, I spilled coffee at my workstation and as I cleaned it up, I hit all sorts of knobs and switches, completely screwing up my settings. The whole time, a recording was running, so I was in a hurry to get things back to normal, so I put the headphones on and as I fidgeted with the controls, I heard a word! I knew something was there!"

He paused to take a breath and finally focused his attention on Lisa. Her appearance took him aback.

"Oh my God. I'm so sorry. Were you sleeping? And here I am, rattling off like a crazed lunatic."

She reached for his arm and said, quietly, "Shhh. It's OK. Do you mind if we just sit?" Not waiting for a response, she was already moving to resume her position on the couch.

Following, he joined her and put his arm around her, drawing her close. "Are you OK? Do you need anything?"

"I'm fine. I just need some more rest."

"You've been working non-stop for weeks. It's not surprising that it's caught up with you. By the way, is your phone off? I've been trying to call you."

"Yes. Sorry. I just needed some undisturbed quiet time."

"No problem."

They sat on the couch, his arm around her shoulder and their heads bent towards each other's, hers resting on his. Her breath fell into a steady rhythm with which he was familiar. Knowing that she was sleeping, he maneuvered so he could comfortably carry her to the bed without disturbing her slumber. As they approached the bedroom, she stirred in his arms, without waking fully, and mumbled something.

"I can't. I won't. It's a mutilation of my work."

Concerned, Stephan whispered, "What's that?"

Instead of answering, she settled in his arms and resumed the steady breathing pattern which indicated sleep. Gently, he put her in bed and covered her. Watching for a moment, he turned and exited the room, closing the door behind him. Walking past the dining room table on his way to the kitchen, he thought he noticed the faint blue camera indicator light on her open laptop. As he turned back, the light had gone out before he had a chance to confirm his suspicion.

STEPHAN'S APARTMENT

I had returned home after preparing a meal for Lisa and leaving it in the kitchen, where she could easily find, heat, and eat it. Having also eaten some of it before leaving her apartment, I was not hungry when I got home and, not in the mood for mindless television, decided to see what I could do with my ill-gotten recording. I was tired, but I thought if I was going to risk court martial and jail, I might as well do something with what I'd taken.

Being the sound geek I am, I've dedicated a bedroom in my apartment to electronic equipment of various sizes and complexity. This equipment allowed me to control and analyze the amplitude and frequency of sound. It also permitted me to vary each, as well as to apply different filters in an attempt to remove interference or background noise. The equipment was available to anybody willing to spend money to obtain it. It was, of course, not as sensitive as the equipment available to me at INSCOM, which was at an entirely different level of sophistication.

I took my phone into what I referred to as my "studio," put it in "Do Not Disturb" mode, and plugged it into the computer that I used to control the equipment. Finding the recording in question, I immediately went to the time-stamped spot that I had previously noted and began playback.

Knowing that an underlying message existed provided an extra impetus for me to keep searching. The settings on my home equipment were not optimized for the current recording, so I fiddled around with them in hopes of coming upon the correct combination. My efforts were rewarded by constant static. It filled my room and reverberated through my head. I turned knobs, slid slides, and switched switches, all with no meaningful change to the noise bombarding my ears. After an hour and a half of frustration, I took a break. I stretched and walked around, all the while contemplating the problem of breaking through the noise. I was drinking a glass of water while standing at the kitchen sink and, having drunk my fill, poured the rest down the drain. As I did, the sight reminded me of the cascading liquid coming from my work desk and keyboard. I had a thought, crazy as it seemed even to me, and returned to my home office. Sitting in front of the keyboard and monitor, I played the recording and pretended to have spilled liquid in the same manner I had at work. I ran my hand over the various controls in random patterns, as if wiping up a spill. This allowed for combinations of controls to occur that I would never have thought to attempt. With the sound blaring from the speakers, I continued my maniacal movements. No change, until suddenly, there was. I immediately lifted my hands and concentrated on the sound. The static still existed, but behind it, very faintly, I could make out what had to be words. I paused the recording and ran it back, being careful not to touch any of the adjustments, then hit play. An obviously mechanically altered voice said:

"u vas yest' ogranichennoye vremya dlya zaversheniya (you have a limited time to complete)"

"Yes!"

I couldn't help but pump my fist, even though the static had resumed, drowning out whatever came next. Noting the settings of each separate aspect of the equipment, I ran the recording back, slowly revising the readouts, all to no avail. Although I could no longer retrieve the first word I had heard earlier, based on the placement of what I had just listened to and what I had heard at work, I surmised that the statement said, "you have a limited time to complete your mission." I kept at it for another forty-five minutes until I heard what seemed to be random sounds: beeps, buzzes, hisses, and musical notes. Something about those struck me as funny, not in a "ha-ha" way, but a "what the fuck" way. As I concentrated on the sounds, I also adjusted my equipment and determined that the sounds were behind the static, as if someone had inserted the static as a masking agent. If that were the case, the sounds meant something. Otherwise, why try to hide them? As I continued to listen on a loop, no discernible pattern jumped at me. Tiring, I took another break, hopeful that being away from the problem would prove fruitful.

After my break had concluded, my hopes were dashed, so I disconnected the phone, shut down the open apps, turned off the equipment, and called it a night.

•　　•　　•

I awoke feeling rested, with the remnants of a dream teasing the edges of my conscious mind. I'm not great at remembering my dreams, except, of course, for the recurring nightmare, which I'd just as soon forget. But this morning, I recalled having dreamt something about the school reunion I'd attended with Lisa. Nothing in particular, so I thought, until an image of the Headmaster onstage popped into my head. I thought it was the Headmaster, although my recollection of his appearance in the dream differed from that in real life. In the dream, he appeared more sinister. It occurred to me that my mind had changed his appearance to that of Ming the Merciless from those old *Flash Gordon* movies which I used to watch with my father. When the movies had been made, Ming was viewed as the most villainous of villains, even though by today's standards he may seem pretty tame. Anyway, in the dream, the Headmaster/Ming wielded Ming's death ray gadget and threatened those in attendance with death by disintegration. A horrible way to die, or so I would imagine. I laughed at the image and, as this was my day off from work, made myself a hearty breakfast.

After breakfast, I called to check on Lisa. This time she answered the phone, which I took as a good sign. She still sounded tired, but in better spirits. She told me her parents were coming over today, so I thought it best to let them have some privacy. The free time would allow me to take care of various errands and other personal matters which required my leaving the apartment, which I did shortly thereafter.

•   •   •

That afternoon, after having completed my personal assignments, I returned to my den of sound geekdom to resume my investigation. I connected my phone to the equipment, opened the appropriate apps, and got back to work on the recording. The settings remained as they had been when I shut down last night, meaning they were set for me to dissect the random sounds I had uncovered beneath the static. As soon as I hit play, the sounds erupted through the speakers, filling the room. Strangely, the static had dissipated to a dull hiss, barely heard. I let the recording play and discovered that the sounds repeated on a loop. When it stopped, I took it back to the spot where I had begun and did it all over again. This time, as it played, I made adjustments which I thought might bring some clarity, changing the overall tonality, frequency and amplitude. While it made certain of the sounds more palatable to the ear and others more annoying, I could find nothing hidden behind them, which meant, in my estimation, that they were the main attraction. I did it for a third time, again making minor adjustments and finding nothing of great import. Until I did, for at some point I turned a dial and slid a slide and heard music. Not just any music, but *La Voltaire et La Franklein*. At first, I had no idea to what I was listening, but knew that somewhere, at some time, I had heard it before. Puzzled, I took my phone off the table and looked at the app on which recorded items had been stored. I usually labeled my recordings for ease of retrieval, and was shocked to discover that, instead of listening to my stolen Homeland Security recording, I had been listening to the recording I had made for Lisa at the reunion.

"What the fuck?"

It totally stumped me. I thought, *"How could I have mixed the two recordings together?"* It shouldn't have been possible unless I knowingly set out to do it. Going back to the app, I found the one labeled simply, "Russian." I thought it would be better than calling it "The Stolen Homeland Security Recording," just in case somebody went through my phone. I plugged the phone back into the equipment, opened the "Russian" recording to where I had left off, and played it. Instantly, the random beeps, buzzes, hisses, and musical notes filled the room. I touched nothing as I listened, trying to recall the sounds I had heard on the reunion recording. To my memory and trained ear, they sounded identical.

I needed to be certain. I copied what I heard on the Homeland recording onto a file on my computer. Then I copied the reunion recording onto a separate file. My equipment allowed me to overlay one on top of the other to analyze any differences. I stared uncomprehendingly at the results.

Identical.

To say it confused me would be an understatement of epic proportions. I stared at the results again, trying to not even blink, lest I miss something that might magically occur. After endless minutes, nothing changed. I played them at the same time and could not hear any difference in timing, tone, frequency or any other measurement of any import.

I stood and walked around my apartment, trying to come up with a viable theory as to how this could be possible. There was absolutely no connection between the two. Right? Unless there was. I couldn't fathom what that connection could be, but, as Spock said, *"If you eliminate the impossible, whatever remains, however improbable, must be the truth."*

With Spock's words ringing in my head, I returned to the equipment and recalled the reunion recording. I adjusted the settings and started the recording at the beginning. I heard Headmaster Payne's speech, together with the background music, *La Voltaire et La Franklein.* As I listened, I couldn't hear any trace of the random noises, but I recalled the look of rapt attention on each of the graduates' faces. I went back to the beginning of the recording and made adjustments until the music of *La Voltaire et La Franklein* was no longer audible, leaving only the beeps, buzzes, hisses, and random musical notes to be heard.

"Damn! *La Voltaire et La Franklein* is only there to mask the star of the show!"

Why? I needed more time to put this together. Recalling what I had heard in the Homeland recording, I realized that time may not be on my side.

"Shit! How are these connected?"

I got up to think someplace else, hoping a change of scenery would help, as I thought, "*That Spock guy sure is smart. I wish he were here now.*"

UNITED GENETICS RESEARCH LAB

Getting ready to head home after a long frustrating day, Jennifer was packing her things and about to leave when a messenger magically appeared at her doorway. She motioned him forward and wordlessly accepted the envelope he handed her as the messenger silently vanished through the open door.

"Now what? They can't be sending me extra work at this hour, can they?"

Since having received the middle-of-the-night telephone call, her mood at and about work had taken a turn for the worse. No announcement had yet been made about Lisa's triumph, but she had no reason to doubt the accuracy of the information her mysterious caller had provided. She chose to accept it as truth, and it would color her every decision moving forward.

With the envelope in hand, she examined it for clues as to its origins. Finding none, she resignedly opened it and allowed the contents to fall onto her desk. A flash drive, followed by a gently floating piece of paper which landed on the desk, exposing a single word: *Private.*

Glancing up at her door and peering through the window into her lab, she determined she was alone enough to chance a peek at the paper. Her hand shook slightly as she picked it up and turned it over to read: *Proof regarding our conversation. We'll be in touch.*

"Hmm."

Placing the flash drive in the palm of her hand, she was tempted to insert it into an available port on her computer, and tentatively reached to do so, when a voice in her head chimed in, *"Not a good idea, Jennifer. It's better to do this on your home computer where you have less chance of being interrupted by surprise or alert any internal computer security at work."*

She determined to listen to her inner voice and exerted the effort it took to pull her hand back and away from the computer port. She nodded assent to herself as she instead placed the drive and note into her purse.

"This should make for an interesting evening," she said to the room, rose from her chair, and exited.

•　　•　　•

Secured in her apartment, the chain and deadbolt lock having been engaged, Jennifer tried to calm herself by pretending that there was nothing of interest in her purse awaiting her. She changed out of her work clothes, put on comfortable sweats, and poured herself a glass of dark red wine. Casually, she strolled to her purse, glass of wine in hand, and fished for the flash drive and note. Both of the items under control, she walked unhurriedly to her computer, which awaited her in the second bedroom office. On the way, she turned the note over in her hand, searching the front and back for clues as to the identity of its sender. She didn't expect to uncover anything and was not overly disappointed to find her expectations met.

Ensconced at the desk, she fired up the computer. While waiting for the electronics to do what they were designed to do, her legs bounced up and down in anticipation, belying her anxiety at what awaited her. At last, the computer was ready to accept her offering as she reverently inserted the drive into the waiting portal.

Sipping from her wineglass, she watched as the file directory appeared on her monitor. The file names meant nothing to her, so she clicked on a random icon and waited for it to open. Scrolling, she couldn't quite believe what had been gifted to her. Eyes opening wide as if to take in the information in one fell swoop, she said, "Holy shit! These are Lisa's notes." Continuing to scroll through the files, she clicked on the icons in order and quickly perused the information.

"Why, that brilliant little bitch. That's how she did it."

Confronted by Lisa's notes, she was able to understand how the mind behind the work fought through the multiple problems the research presented. Reluctantly, she admitted to herself that, even given another year, she wouldn't have come upon the solution which Lisa had uncovered.

"OK. I'm impressed."

She sat back in her chair, wine glass at her lips, as a pang of conscience found its way into a portion of her mind she thought had been under total control.

"*So, what do I do with this*?" she thought.

As she was running various scenarios through her somewhat troubled mind, her ever-present cell phone vibrated on the desk. Looking at it, she noted a "Blocked Call."

Deep in thought, she said to herself, "I'm not answering a blocked call."

Ignoring the vibrations, she continued to contemplate the dilemma. At last, the vibrating stopped, and she was free to once again ponder the issue and its moral implications. She had been good friends with, and a co-worker of, Lisa for years. She genuinely enjoyed her company. How could she even consider a betrayal of these proportions? What did that say about her and her drive to get ahead? How was she even considering it? She had almost come to the conclusion she would ignore what they had given her and tell Lisa what had happened when her phone both rang and vibrated.

"What the hell? I turned the ringer off."

Confused, she looked at the phone and once again noted a "Blocked Call."

"This is bizarre."

Finally, she realized. "*Oh, shit. What if it's him?*"

She connected the call and said, hesitantly, "Hello?"

A mechanically altered voice replied, "I take it you've received our gift."

"I have."

"And did you find it interesting?"

"I did."

"That's good. I thought you might."

Silence, as both parties waited for the other to continue. Her anxiety getting the better of her, Jennifer was the first to blink, metaphorically speaking.

"What do you expect me to do with the information?"

Bemused, the voice answered, "We expect nothing. We have a proposition which you are free to accept or reject, as you see fit."

As she opened her mouth to respond, she felt exasperation creep into her voice. Wanting to keep it under control, she took a silent breath and said, "OK. What's your proposition?"

"We would like you to use her research for a slightly different purpose."

Unable to contain herself any longer, Jennifer succumbed to the exasperation and said, "Please, stop with the games and just tell me what you want."

"Very well. As I'm sure you are aware, the research can be put to use in more ways than one. What Lisa did was find a way to target specific gene therapy for specific genetic diseases. The opposite is also a possibility."

Letting that sink in, it took Jennifer a moment to respond.

"Are you talking about targeting specific diseases for specific genes?"

"Ah, I'm glad you got there on your own. It shows the promise we had hoped for."

Jennifer struggled to be more in control of herself and said, "Are you asking me to create a disease targeted at a specific person?"

"Yes. Do you have a problem with that?"

Remembering the previous bout with her conscience, she was slow to reply. When she did, she said, "A little, yes."

"If you're unable to get past your moral objection, we'll pretend that you never saw the information, this conversation never occurred, and we'll have to find someone else, although that would be an inconvenience, for both of us."

The threat was veiled, but present, nonetheless. Jennifer realized that whomever she was dealing with had power and, based on what she'd been presented, was not afraid to use it. It caused her to rethink her position.

"If I agree to do this," she said, "what's in it for me?"

"Ah, the crux of the decision making-process rears its head," an amused individual responded. "You would receive credit for the greatest medical discovery of the generation. How you benefit from that would be entirely up to you."

Enticed by the possibility of fame and fortune, she asked, "And what about Lisa? Do you think she'll just sit idly by and let me take the accolades for her work?"

"You won't have to worry about Lisa. We'll have that under control."

Silence hung between them.

"So, are you in or not?" asked the voice.

"I'm in," was the simple reply.

"Good. We'll have your first target for you in the next day or so. Let's call it a proof of concept. We'll be in touch."

The call disconnected, leaving Jennifer alone with her thoughts. At first, that portion of her mind containing a conscience had once again been activated. However, it didn't last long. As was her way, the inner rationalization process was swift and complete.

"What the hell! In for a penny, in for a pound," already dreaming of the accolades and untold rewards to come.

LISA'S APARTMENT

"Would you like a cup of tea, dear?" Roxanne asked her daughter.

"No thanks, Mom. I'm good for now."

Lisa was relaxed on her couch, still haggard looking, but definitely on the mend. Her parents, worried about her, had come over to check for themselves, video chatting not being sufficient to put their minds at ease. And for good reason. On a call, Lisa had been able to maneuver her appearance in such a way as to appear to be in better shape than she was. Her parents, being no strangers to deception, thought it best to get a first-hand look.

Peter was sitting on a chair near the sofa, trying not to be obvious while observing his daughter. He was pretending to read a newspaper, glancing over the top in what he hoped was a stealthy manner.

"Dad, you know I can see you looking over the top of the paper. Why don't you just put it down?"

Embarrassed at having been discovered, Peter slowly folded the newspaper and placed it on the coffee table.

"Look, I know you're both worried about me, but, really, I'm fine."

"So, you're ready to get out and go back to work?" asked Peter.

"Well, not just yet," replied Lisa.

"Dear, what's going on? Really. You can tell us. Maybe we can help," implored Roxanne. "You look as if you haven't slept for weeks. Are you having trouble sleeping? Maybe we can get you something to help with that."

"No, Mom, sleeping isn't the issue. I sleep like the dead. It's just that I can't seem to get enough. No matter how much I sleep, I'm still exhausted."

"Have you gone to a doctor?" an even more concerned Roxanne asked.

"No."

"Well, don't you think it would be a good idea? Let me make an appointment for you," Roxanne persisted.

Lisa opened her mouth to respond, thought better of it, and snapped it shut, choosing to remain quiet. Peter, watching his daughter like a hawk looking for sustenance, noticed.

"You were about to say something. What is it?"

"Nothing. It wasn't important," was Lisa's reply.

Peter responded, "So, which is it? Nothing or not important? It can't be both."

Knowing how her father can get once he dug his heels into something, she looked to her mother for support, but found only concern. Resigned, she gave in to the inevitable.

"It's just a feeling that I have. Nothing specific. I sleep and sleep, and yet, when I wake up, I have the strange feeling that something's missing."

Roxanne, concerned, looked around the room. "Do you think someone's been stealing from you?"

Smiling, Lisa said, "No, Mom. Not like that." Gathering her thoughts, she continued. "It's like I can't remember chunks of time…"

Before she could continue, Peter jumped in and said, "Do you have amnesia? That could be serious."

"No, Dad, not amnesia. Let me finish," said an exasperated Lisa.

"Sorry. Go on."

"Like I said, it seems that I can't remember chunks of time, and then, suddenly, the memory will come back to me."

Relieved, Roxanne said, "Oh, that doesn't sound very serious."

Continuing, Lisa said, "Maybe. It's just that when I get the memory back, it just seems wrong."

Leaning forward, elbows on knees, Peter asked, "Wrong how?"

"It's like the memory isn't real. Like something happened, or I did something or went somewhere, but what I remember is something different from what happened in reality."

Both parents were stunned into silence, as they could do nothing but stare at their daughter.

"I know it sounds weird, and I know that can't be the case. It's just a weird feeling I can't explain. Maybe I'm just overtired. Maybe I have mono." To put her parents at ease, she said, "I'll go have that checked."

"Really?" asked Roxanne.

"Really."

Lisa got up from her seat on the couch and said, "You know, I think I'll have that tea now. I'll put some water on."

As Lisa made her way to the kitchen, Roxanne and Peter were left alone, each deep in their own private thoughts. Finally, Peter turned to Roxanne and said, "What do you think?"

"I don't know. If this were another place and another time, I'd have serious suspicions. But not here and not now. It's not possible," said Roxanne in a manner which clearly indicated she was looking for assurance.

"I agree," answered Peter. To himself he thought, *But damn, it is suspicious.*

Unseen by any of them, the faint blue light on Lisa's computer slowly faded out.

A HOMELAND SECURITY LIMOUSINE

"You're living the high-life," commented Dan as he searched his surroundings while settling into the spacious back seat of the limousine.

Laughing, Bob Ferguson joined his guest in admiring the car's interior. "And all at the taxpayer's expense. Ain't life grand?"

Ferguson pushed one of the many buttons at his disposal and the car pulled smoothly away from the curb.

"The car is clean, I presume?" asked Dan.

"What do you think?" a smiling Ferguson asked.

"I had to ask."

"Touché," responded Bob, remembering their last phone conversation.

Dan indicated acceptance of the unspoken compliment by nodding his head, and said, "So, we're in a rolling, and, I presume, bulletproof 'Cone of Silence.' What's on your mind?"

"One of these days, you're going to actually engage in small talk and I'm going to have to be rushed to the ER."

"I'm only looking out for your health, Bob. I'd hate to see that happen."

"Right." Pausing, Ferguson opened a nearby hidden panel and removed a cold bottle of water. He offered it to Dan, who shook his head and declined the offer. "Suit yourself," replied Bob as he twisted open the cap and took a long, satisfying drink. His thirst satiated, he continued. "OK. After hearing about your encounter with our old friends at 1789, I thought you might be interested in getting back into the game. I know you're beginning to go stir-crazy."

"Back into the game, how?"

"As a director at Homeland Security, I have, shall we say, some leeway in hiring. I find I could use an assistant and, being familiar with your skill-set from our previous experiences together, thought you'd be perfect."

"And which aspect of my 'skill-set' would you be most interested in?"

"The aspect that respects confidentiality and puts your country before personal gain or relationships."

"It sounds as if you're more interested in loyalty than skill-sets."

"It may sound like that, but believe me, one without the other is useless. I know how your mind works and what you believe is best for this country right now. I think I know what you're willing to do to make your vision a reality. A vision which, by the way, I believe we share. That being said, if you agree, I'd like to bring you aboard as a special attaché or agent. You'd report directly to me. And to clarify, that means *only* to me."

Ferguson stopped his sales pitch to sit back and watch his former boss as he mulled over what he'd just heard. What he saw on Fowler's face was a blank canvass, giving nothing away, which was exactly what he'd hoped, expected, to see.

"So, what do you say, Dan?"

"What I gather from what you've said, and more so from what you haven't said, and based on where we're having this conversation and your complete lack of actual information, is that you're working on something that is not sanctioned by the powers that be at Homeland."

Ferguson remained silent, hoping that he had become as skilled at revealing nothing as his former boss.

"Based on our past relationship and what I know about your political views, and the fact you want me to report only to you, I'm also assuming that the fewer people who know about whatever you have cooking, the better. As you know, that's the way I like it."

"So, in or out, Dan?"

"Do I get more information so I can make an educated assessment?"

"Once you sign the confidentiality documents and come on board, you get to see everything I have."

Pretending to think about the offer, Dan looked out the window and waited a few beats before holding his hand out, as if to receive something. "Let's get this signed up."

Smiling, Ferguson reached for the briefcase sitting on the seat next to him, opened it, and removed a sheaf of papers attached to a clipboard to which a pen had been attached for easy signing.

Returning the smile, Dan reached for the clipboard and said, "You seem pretty sure of yourself."

"As somebody once taught me, it's always good to be prepared," replied Bob, as he sat back and watched his new agent sign the documents without bothering to read them.

The task completed, Fowler handed the clipboard back to his new boss and said, "What have you got?"

Reaching back into his briefcase, Ferguson removed a large envelope and handed it to his new agent. "I'm going to have to ask that you review this while we're driving around. Take as much time as you need. I can work from here while you read."

Accepting the envelope, Agent Fowler removed the documents, sat back, and began his review.

STEPHAN AT WORK

Try as I might, I could not put together a realistic scenario in which the Homeland recording and the reunion recording were connected. They occurred at different times. The Homeland recording had been intercepted using state-of-the-art spy equipment. I made the reunion recording using my cell phone, under my control. Coming up with some science fiction, time warp, atmospheric anomaly was beyond my conjuring abilities. I knew there had to be some connection, as there was no way it could be a random coincidence, but as to what that connection was, I was totally and thoroughly stumped. Damn you, Spock!

I was at INSCOM. I had headphones on, and other intercepted recordings playing, but my concentration was adrift. No matter what I was listening to, my mind came back to the strange confluence of those recordings. Trying to channel Spock, I attempted to use logic, something that us mere humans rarely embrace by itself. As some Russian words played through my headset, and I continued to ignore them, I delved into what I thought of as logic to find a connection.

If the sounds hidden behind *La Voltaire et La Franklein* and those found on the Homeland recording were the same, and I believed they were, one commonality had to be their origin. So, which was created first? I no longer had access to the original Homeland recording, it having been returned to the Department of Homeland Security. I did, however, have my phone. As surreptitiously as possible, I removed the phone from my pocket and brought it to my desk. I pretended to fiddle with my computer controls and opened the app on my phone where the contraband recording had been stored. Then, I reviewed the information that had accompanied the recording. I noted that the date of interception was after the reunion. Staring at the ceiling, it occurred to me that, while interesting, it didn't really serve my purpose. The sounds might have been created that day or twenty years before. Disappointed, I returned the phone to my pocket and again pretended to listen to the words being fed into my head. Having my eyes closed wouldn't arouse any suspicion, as it was how I worked. I closed my eyes and concentrated, blocking out the noise coming through my headset.

La Voltaire et La Franklein. I thought that, since it had been so prominently played at the reunion, it must be the theme song for the school. Okay. Was it written for the school? I thought not, but needed to do some research to be certain. Conjecture was not a solid basis on which to proceed. I opened my eyes and looked at the computer in front of me. As state-of-the-art as it might have been, it was a single purpose piece of technology. It allowed no access to the internet. Frustrated, I removed my headphones and threw them onto my desk. I stood and stretched, which occasioned the appearance of Corporal Clark's face slowly appearing over the top of the cubicle divider as if attached to a hydraulic lift.

"What's up, Sarge?"

"How is it you can always hear me when you're supposed to have headphones glued to your ears?"

"In case you hadn't noticed, I'm an extremely talented individual."

"Talented at mischief."

Smiling, Corporal Clark said, "At that, too." Waiting for a retort from me and being disappointed, he said, "You seem out of sorts today. Everything all right?"

One thing I could always say about Corporal Clark is that he was always perceptive.

"Yeah. I'm just a little preoccupied with something."

"Something having to do with that Homeland recording?"

I glanced around to make certain that no other prying ears were peeping over a cubicle wall before I answered. "You must practice voodoo or some other dark art." I moved closer and lowered my voice even more. "There are some anomalies I'm trying to work through and I can't seem to concentrate on anything else."

"Well, you better get your act together. We need to get our reports filed on today's recordings before we head out. Why don't you come to my place after work and we can try to work through it?"

Considering, I said, "I just might do that. Thanks."

He nodded, and the hydraulic lift descended.

•   •   •

The thought of having company after work, surprisingly, seemed like a good idea. Joel was always very companionable. He matched my penchant for sound-geekdom with his own penchant for computer geekdom. Based on where I found myself in my current dilemma, I felt it would be beneficial to bounce some ideas off somebody else, especially someone with computer skills. Who knew where it could lead?

We picked up a pizza on the way to his place and I followed him home. I'd been there before, but rarely and not recently enough to be certain where it was. We pulled into the parking area of a large apartment complex, which consisted of five separate five-story buildings. He was on the fourth floor of building number three. Once inside, he grabbed a couple of beers from the refrigerator and we dug into the meat-lovers pies. No healthy vegetables for this duo. As we ate, I filled him in on the generalities of what I'd been dealing with. I didn't want to give him too much specific information because I wanted to ensure that he maintained at least a semblance of plausible deniability. After all, I had technically broken the law by recording the Homeland interception and, if the shit hit the fan, I wanted to keep his splatter to a minimum. He listened to what I had to say as we devoured the pizza. After finishing our meal, we removed the empty box and cans and sat back down.

"So," he began, "let me get this straight. You have two recordings from two different times and two different sources. There is no apparent connection between the two, other than a set of identical sounds hidden in the background of each. Is that a concise summary?"

Impressed, I responded with a simple, "Yes."

He sat back as he looked at me and began a quiet conversation with himself. Most of it was too quiet for me to hear, but after a few minutes, he sat up and said, "I think I might have something that could help."

"Great!" was my enthusiastic reply.

"But," he quickly interjected, "there is something you should know first." His tone placed me on high alert.

"Ohhhh...kay." I drew the word out, unsure where this was going. I waited as he made an internal decision.

"The program which I'm proposing we use," he began, "may be, how shall I put it, slightly less than legal."

"Slightly less than legal," I parroted. I sat staring at him for a moment before laughing.

"What's funny?" he asked.

"You're worried about using a 'slightly less than legal' program on sounds I illegally recorded from a Homeland Security interception."

"You...what?!?" After digesting what I'd just told him, he, too, laughed. "Well, aren't we the outlaws?"

"Yeah. We're the Hole in the Head Gang. What the hell. Let's do it."

He nodded his assent, rose from his chair, and headed for his array of computers as he said, "Maybe we can have adjoining prison cells."

So much for plausible deniability.

•　　•　　•

We did some basic research on *La Voltaire et La Franklein*, just to be certain that it wasn't something created for the school. We discovered it had been written in the 18th century to commemorate a meeting between Benjamin Franklin and Voltaire, the writer, historian, and philosopher. At this discovery, I looked at Joel and said, "Who knew?"

"Definitely not these two rubes," was his response.

Having dispensed with that formality, Joel said, "I'm going to need the recording of those sounds."

Part of me knew this request was inevitable. Still, I hesitated. This was my last chance to keep him out of whatever I was getting into. He noticed my hesitation and intuited the reason.

"I'm a big boy and can make my own decisions, Sarge. I'm willing to live with the consequences."

As I said, the dark arts.

I retrieved my phone and pulled up the recordings. He connected the phone to his computer and uploaded both separate collections of sounds. He overlayed and played them back.

"As you said. Identical," confirming my previous conclusion.

I nodded in agreement.

"OK. This next part is where it gets dodgy, from a legal standpoint. It's also going to take some time, so don't inspect instant gratification."

"I do like my instant gratification, but I'll get over it."

He smiled and said, "I'm going to do a broad search through various databases. I'll search for the same, or at least similar, groupings of sounds. The search is going to encompass not only our government's classified recording files, but those of most governments of the world. That is a lot of information to access and analyze. Because I don't have a super-computer powering the search, and because it takes time to penetrate the defenses trying to stop just such an incursion, I figure we have at least 4 or 5 days to wait for a result."

"Where the hell...?" I stopped myself. "Never mind. I really don't want to know."

"You probably don't," he responded.

His finger poised over the "Enter" key on his keyboard, he looked at me for final approval and, when I nodded, plunged us into the next phase of whatever this was.

No turning back now.

ROXANNE'S HOUSE

With Peter away on business, Roxanne was looking forward to a quiet day at home. She relaxed on her living room couch and read a new book she had recently picked up from her local library. A steaming cup of freshly brewed coffee rested on the table on which her feet were propped. The aroma filled her nostrils and brought a smile of pleasure to her lips. She rarely allowed herself to dwell on the past, especially those days of her childhood in the Soviet Union, but the smell of the coffee was a trigger her mind could not ignore.

Roxanne had lived in a hovel with her parents and three siblings, of which she was the youngest. The icy wind blew through the cracks in the walls, almost unabated, making winters torturous. The family often huddled together in the morning, gathered around the wood-burning stove for warmth, while her mother prepared what she used to pretend was coffee in the family's prized cezve, the long-handled pot with a pouring lip seen so often in Turkish coffee houses.

Roxanne lifted her coffee cup to her nose and inhaled deeply. Taking a sip of the hot liquid, she remembered... *the bitter taste of the chicory root and barley concoction her mother used to brew. Coffee was in short supply in the Soviet Union in those days, and what supply there was usually found its way to high-ranking politicians, not the peasants huddled together in the countryside.*

Inevitably, and the reason she didn't allow herself to dwell on the past, her thoughts rushed to the day on which... *the Soviet military came to her village in search of suitable candidates for a project that would "propel the Motherland to the forefront of the world and destroy the imperialist West." Her parents didn't know enough to hide their youngest daughter, so when the knock on the door came, a baby-faced Leonid Pushkin strode into the room uninvited, looked around, and pointed at the young girl cowering behind her mother.*

"Comrades, you have been given the highest of honors. Your daughter has been chosen to represent the Soviet Union in a most important endeavor."

Roxanne's mother pushed her daughter farther behind her, as her father stepped forward to address the uniformed intruder.

"Sir, I assure you that my daughter is too young to be of any service to Mother Russia. Please, take me instead. It would be my honor to serve my country again."

Young Pushkin drew his eyes away from the girl, looked her father up and down as if inspecting a hog for butchering, and scoffed, "You are too old and useless to be of service." Turning his attention to Roxanne's mother, he said, "We will be back in fifteen minutes. Gather her belongings and have her ready to go. We will post a guard outside of your door. In honor of your sacrifice, the State will provide you with a slab of bacon and a bag of coffee." Without further discussion, Pushkin turned and exited the shack, leaving a guard at the door, as promised.

Coffee. So many mixed memories accompanied the aroma.

•   •   •

The ringing of the doorbell abruptly brought Roxanne back to the present. It took her a moment to reacquire her bearings, so the doorbell rang again before she could make her way to the peephole. Once at the door, she gazed through the fish-eyed lens and saw a young man wearing the brown uniform of a UPS driver. She shifted her focus and saw the brown van parked on the street, the UPS logo prominently displayed. Before opening the door, one hand discreetly went into the pocket of her jeans, her fingers wrapping around the folded switchblade knife that made its home there. With her free hand, she opened the door and greeted the waiting messenger with a beaming smile.

"Yes?"

The messenger looked at the package and then up at Roxanne. "Good morning. Mrs. Jones?"

"Yes."

The man nodded and held out an electronic pad. "Please sign here," indicating the correct location.

Roxanne accepted the stylus, signed where shown as he continued to hold the pad, and returned the stylus to the driver, who then handed her a small box clad in plain brown paper and encircled in twine.

She accepted the package, said "Thank you," and closed the door. Sporting a puzzled look as she retreated to the kitchen, she placed the package onto a counter and, removing her hand from her pocket, now clutching the folded knife, expertly flicked the blade open and cut the string binding the package. She placed the knife on the counter next to the package and carefully tore away the brown paper, revealing an elaborate white box decorated with what appeared to be gold filigree. Noticing a small card, she pulled it from the envelope and saw the logo of the animal shelter where she and Peter would occasionally volunteer.

She let out a breath and relaxed. Even after all the years she'd spent in the United States, the feeling in the pit of her stomach when something unexpected happened came unbidden. Maybe it was all those years of training from such a young age, but the paranoia always remained.

She walked to the living room to retrieve her now tepid cup of coffee. She placed it in the microwave and heated it up enough to cause the steam to once again fill her nostrils before taking a deep drink. The caffeine shouldn't help to calm her nerves, but somehow it did.

She approached the box once again, removed the lid, and saw an attractive bottle with an elaborate squeeze bulb atomizer on top. Once again, a note awaited, this time without the envelope. She picked it up and saw that it had been handwritten, although no signature accompanied it.

"This fragrance has been especially created for Roxanne Jones. We hope you enjoy it. To fully appreciate the fragrance, please spray the perfume in the air

twice and inhale deeply. Thereafter, spray a bit onto your wrists. Thank you for all your help."

"How thoughtful," thought Roxanne. She picked up the bottle, noticing the unexpected heft of what appeared to be crystal. "I wonder how they can afford something like this," she thought, as she followed the handwritten directions. "Lovely," she said aloud. As she grabbed her coffee cup and retreated to the solitude of her book, she thought, "I hope Peter likes it."

LISA'S LAB

Lisa had finally gotten back to work, having mostly recovered from what felt to her like a debilitating bout of strange dreams, uneven sleep, and what she had self-diagnosed as slight depression. She found being back in the lab reassuring and was beginning to feel more like herself as the day went on. She'd had a pleasant lunch with Jennifer, who had told her she knew about her accomplishment and how proud she was of her and her amazing achievement. While she appreciated Jennifer's kind words, she found them to be slightly out of character. Jennifer had never been a gracious loser. Perhaps her friend was maturing. Still, it got Lisa's inner antennae up, at least a bit. Maybe her paranoia was just the vestige of whatever she'd been going through since her breakthrough, since she was not a paranoid person by nature. In fact, just the opposite. She had always been a trusting soul.

As the day drew to a close, she found herself thinking about calling Stephan, when her cell phone rang. She checked caller ID and smiled, reaching to connect the call.

"I was just thinking about calling you," she said cheerily.

"Really," answered an obviously mechanically altered voice, a hint of amusement evident.

Lisa checked caller ID, just to make certain that it showed Stephan, before saying, "Who is this, and what are you doing with Stephan's phone?" The paranoia had taken two steps forward.

"Lisa, stop being so naïve," responded the voice. "We can make caller ID show anybody we want. This isn't Stephan's phone. I just knew you'd answer a call from him."

The paranoia was now front and center. Tentatively, she asked, "Who is this?"

Instead of answering, the voice said, "You've always shown a remarkable resistance to your training, even from an early age. We always thought it was the price for such a remarkable initial adaptation to that same training."

"What the hell are you talking about?" Lisa was thoroughly confused.

"Lisa, I know you have no memory of your early training. That, too, was part of the training. But the response to your programming was still remarkable. We know you've just gone through a difficult time. Not remembering certain things, thinking that some memories were false. That is truly remarkable. No other subject had come close to such a conclusion. But time is now short. We tried to use your programming to fulfill the next stage of our plan, but your mind refused to cooperate."

Lisa interrupted the voice. "You're out of your mind. Either that, or this is some elaborate prank being instituted by some giant asshole. I think I'll go with the asshole hypothesis."

Laughing, the voice continued, "Think what you will. At this stage, what you think is not important. What *is* important is that you cooperate. To ensure your cooperation, we've sent a gift to your mother. When we're done with this call, you should call her. Ask if she's received a package that was specially prepared for her. It will appear to have come from an animal shelter which she and your father volunteer at. So American of them! Ask her how she liked the fragrance."

"What have you done?"

"Just call and ask her. If she confirms, then you will know your research has already been used to target the holder of specific DNA, in this case with Huntington's disease."

Shaking with fear, she said, "You bastard." She paused, deep in thought. "What the hell? Now I have a faint recollection of being asked to create a DNA specific disease."

"Which you, somehow, refused to do, even with all of your programming."

"You keep talking about programming, but I still have no idea what you're talking about."

"Perhaps someday I or one of my associates will tell you. For now, we need you to cooperate and this was the only way to assure that."

"If somebody has already weaponized it, why do you need me and why do you need to infect my mother?" she asked, a hitch in her voice as she began to lose control of her emotions.

"Let's just say we have our reasons. Call your mother. And don't bother to tell anybody about this conversation, unless, of course, you'd like to make them a target as well. We'll be in touch."

The mysterious person on the other end abruptly disconnected the call. She placed the phone on her desk and thought about what she'd just heard. Shaking with both fear and indignation, she called her mother.

A HOMELAND SECURITY LIMOUSINE (CONTINUED)

The newly anointed Agent Fowler took his time reviewing the files, not wanting to miss anything. After two hours, he refocused his attention on his new boss, who instantly felt the gaze, looked at Fowler, and said, "So?"

"So, that is quite a lot to take in." He paused and gazed out the window, watching as the city's landmarks sped by and he gathered his thoughts. Turning back to Director Ferguson, he said, "After all this time, the Franklin School's been activated? We didn't have nearly this much information back in the day. Where'd you get it?"

"Do you remember Theresa Cook?" asked Ferguson.

Searching through his memory banks, Fowler finally replied, "A teacher in the early days of the school?"

"Excellent memory. Since we had looked into the school early on, and come up empty, I still had my suspicions that it wasn't what it appeared to be, at least not only that. So, I flagged a couple of names, Theresa Cook being one of them. My computer automatically alerted me when she got arrested for a DUI. At first I thought nothing of it. After all, the Franklin School has been, and still is, a well-respected institution. Still, something nagged at me, so I looked into it, just to see what I could see."

"You paid her a visit."

"I did."

"How'd that go?"

Ferguson laid his head back and related the story.

•   •   •

"I got hold of the police station and told them to put her on ice until I could get there. It was a small town, about two hours from here, so, based on my very impressive credentials, the locals were more than happy to cooperate. I arrived at the station about two hours later and talked to the head cop. I instructed him to keep her in lockup for another twenty minutes and then to bring her to an interview room. I told him to have her cuffed and attached to the table, as if she were a hardened criminal that had previously escaped custody."

"Nice touch," interjected Fowler.

Ferguson nodded and continued.

"When they brought her into the room, I was waiting in a chair. I remained silent as they escorted her into the room and cuffed her to the table. It was all I could do not to laugh. Finally, they left us alone, and I observed her silently for a few minutes. She, in turn, studied me. She appeared to be slightly hungover, but she didn't seem like the scared old lady I was anticipating. After a couple of minutes of this, she finally spoke."

"Do I know you?"

"No, I don't believe you do."

"Then what the fuck are you doing here, and why this?" as she tried raising her hands, only to be stopped by the handcuffs.

"You're facing a very serious charge, Ms. Cook. I don't know if you remember, but your vehicle struck a pedestrian who, at the moment, is still alive. But that could change."

I could see her searching her memory. I remained quiet while she did. She looked at me and said, "Bullshit."

I said to the room, "Chief, could you bring the accident report in here, please?"

A moment later, the door opened, the chief entered and handed me a file, which I immediately handed to the prisoner, without even glancing at the contents. She looked through it, flipping pages as best she could while connected to the table. I could see her wonder about whether she had struck a pedestrian and forgotten.

"Had she? Struck a pedestrian, I mean," interjected Fowler.

"No. It was something I concocted with the Chief."

Fowler smiled as Ferguson continued.

"Satisfied?" I asked her.

I could see that the seed of doubt had been planted. Instead of answering, she asked, "So, why is this of so much interest to a Fed?"

I hadn't told her anything about myself, but, I have to admit, it was pretty obvious.

I answered with a question of my own. "You're the Theresa Cook who taught at the Franklin School when it was first established?"

She nodded.

"In that case, I may be able to help you with your current predicament."

"And why would you do that?" she asked.

"Because you may be able to help me with a predicament of my own," was my reply.

"And how's that?"

"I have some questions about the Franklin School and its activities in the 80s."

I could see that my meaning had struck home. She sat a little straighter and said, "I can't talk to you about that, especially here."

"Let's say, hypothetically, that I could have you released, and the charges dropped. Would I be able to count on your cooperation?"

She stared at me, as if to gauge my trustworthiness, and said, "Hypothetically, yes. You could count on that."

I nodded and left the room. I went outside and, about ten minutes later, greeted Ms. Cook, a free woman, on the sidewalk in front of the police station.

"Let's go for a ride, Ms. Cook."

She looked around as if trying to determine if there was any route to use in making an escape attempt. Finding none, she turned to me, descended the stairs, and said, "Let's."

●　　●　　●

"So?" asked Agent Fowler.

"We went for that drive and she told me about the long-term program for the students of the school. She was initially reluctant to go into too much detail, but since they had disbanded the program in the early to mid-aughts, she didn't think it would be an issue. Shortly after the program had been disbanded, she retired to live the quiet life."

"Did you believe her?"

"For the most part, I did. I drove her home, and we said our goodbyes, never to see one another again."

"So, how and why was the program re-instituted?" asked Fowler.

Glancing at his watch, Ferguson said, "That's a tale for another day. I have a previous engagement that I need to leave for now."

As he said this, the car pulled to a curb and glided to a stop. Bob held his hand out and said, "Welcome aboard, Dan. Glad to have you."

Dan accepted the hand and shook it. He opened the car door and exited. As it drove away, he found himself at precisely the same spot where his limo odyssey had begun.

STEPHAN

Late at night on the third day after my dinner at Joel's, I received an excited call from him. He didn't go into much detail. In fact, he didn't go into any detail at all. He merely said, "I have some results that I think you'll find very interesting. I have some things to check out, but it looks really promising. We shouldn't discuss it over the phone. Let's meet after work tomorrow."

"Tomorrow," the day of our scheduled meeting, was Joel's day off, so we arranged to meet at a local restaurant halfway between our respective apartments. He was adamant that we meet in a nondescript public place with plenty of background noise. Due to our jobs, we were well aware of the risks of our conversation being "overheard." We knew that various governmental agencies with "listening" capabilities had certain trigger words that garnered more attention than most people would care for. Based on the scope of the searches that Joel had run, I assumed that our conversation would contain at least a few of those trigger words, so the more we could mask them, the better.

I was able to get some actual work done that day, although I found my mind summoning various scenarios uncovered by Joel's searches. Most seemed like either science fiction or the stuff of fantastic tales. After all, Joel's search had the potential to uncover secrets held by world governments, many of which, we had always been led to believe, were awash in nefarious plots to do us harm. Could he have uncovered the link for which I had been searching? Could he turn out to be my Spock? The more I thought about it, the more anxious I became. So, I forced myself to concentrate on my current assignments, although I couldn't help the occasional glance at the current time, just to gauge how much longer my wait would be.

At last, my workday came to an end. I prepared my reports and submitted them, as required by protocol. Done, I exited the building and hurried to my car. As I drove to the appointed location, I called Lisa, just to check in. When she answered her phone, I had the distinct impression she wasn't expecting me to be on the line, even though I was certain my name would have been displayed on caller ID. As a result, she sounded odd, unlike her usually enthusiastic greeting. She professed that all was well, but it sounded to me as if she were trying to make it seem so, for my benefit. I knew enough not to push too hard, so I didn't. Perhaps I was too wrapped up in my own little drama. In any event, we disconnected our call, and I drove to the rendezvous point, determined to call her later and check how she was doing.

I parked and entered the restaurant. It was dinnertime and packed. It was not the type of place that had a maître d, or even a high schooler seating people. Strictly first-come, first-served. I walked around and, as luck would have it, came upon a family who'd just completed their dinner and was leaving a booth in the back. I quickly staked my claim and sat down facing the door so I could see when Joel arrived. As I sat there, the constant noise created a din that made it hard to hear myself think, let alone hear the person to whom I might be speaking. Immediately, I understood why Joel had chosen this location.

A server approached, and I advised him I was waiting for another person to arrive. So I wasn't taking up the precious space without having anything, I ordered coffee while I waited. As I sat there, I used my cell phone to scroll through emails, check social media, and make certain that we weren't suddenly at war with another nation. I was aware of the dirty looks I was receiving from parties waiting to be seated. I checked the time and discovered that it was thirty minutes past our appointed meeting time. Unlike Joel, but traffic could be a bitch this time of day, so I thought little of it. Another half-hour passed, and still no Joel. Now I thought something was off. I used my cell phone and called him. No answer. Not only no answer, but it went directly to voice mail. Odd. I tried again with the same results. I told myself to give him another fifteen minutes and did just that, constantly checking the time. The fifteen additional minutes having passed, I tried my luck at calling once again. Same results. I made a decision and called the server to my table. I apologized for having taken the table for so long and asked for my check, which I was tendered by the obviously put-off employee. I shrugged, got up, and paid my bill. I dialed the number again in the parking lot, but again it went straight to voice mail. Uncertain what to do, I looked at the parking lot, searching for Joel's car, a black Toyota Celica. I saw plenty of black cars, but not the one for which I was looking. Not knowing what else to do, I walked to my car, thinking about alternatives. I decided I needed to drive to Joel's apartment, and did just that.

The road to his apartment was a major highway. Traffic was heavy, but at least it was moving. I exited the highway and, remembering the way from the other night, drove directly to his apartment complex. I parked, went into the correct building, and rode the elevator to the fourth floor.

As the elevator doors opened, darkness greeted me. Not the darkness of a cave, but the darkness of a hallway lit only by the occasional emergency light. It was dim, with barely enough light to make my way without bumping into a wall. I had stood looking at the hallway so long that the elevator doors began to close. Quickly, I shot my arm forward before they closed and I had to take the ride again. I muttered, "Ow," to myself as the doors smashed into my arm with just a little less force than a guillotine, which caused them to reopen long enough for me to slip through. In the hallway, rubbing the bruise which I was certain would appear at any moment, I let my eyes adjust to the lack of light. Getting my bearings, I turned to my left and slowly made my way to Joel's apartment. Something felt off enough to make me wish I had a weapon. It could have been the lack of lighting, but I thought that the dimness just added to my discomfort and wasn't the cause. I inched my way to the apartment, my ears attuned for the slightest sound that might have been out of the ordinary. I heard nothing. No other tenants making noise in their apartments. No sounds blaring from television sets. Nothing. Now my hackles were definitely up.

I cautiously approached Joel's apartment and stopped beside his door. I stood still, breathing as quietly as possible as I strained my hearing to pick up anything that might alert me to a dangerous situation. After what seemed like an eternity, I reached for the door handle, feeling that knocking would not be appropriate. As I turned the knob, the door gently pushed open, creaking on its unoiled hinges. I held my breath at the sound and waited. I was rewarded with silence.

Advancing, I pushed the door open enough for me to sneak through, entered the apartment, and eased the door closed behind me. I tried a light switch, but was met only with a clicking noise and no light. Could the electricity be out in the building? No, I took the elevator up. Just on this floor? I suppose it was a possibility but, not being an electrician, really had no idea. Thankfully, cell phones were all equipped with a flashlight function, so I utilized mine and shone it into the depths of the apartment.

At first, I didn't comprehend what I was seeing. I thought it looked ransacked, but not in the way one would imagine. Some random drawers were open, and things looked disheveled, but it wasn't completely trashed, as I would have expected. I made my way to the room which housed Joel's computers and came to a complete standstill and just stared. This is where the bulk of whatever happened had happened. I tried to remember what had been there a few days ago. I thought a couple of CPUs were missing, along with at least one laptop. Various papers had been strewn about the table, but a cursory exam showed they had been left behind for a reason. I quickly checked the rest of the apartment for Joel, but found no trace. He wasn't home. I hoped he hadn't been home when whoever had visited had been here.

In the distance, I heard a siren. As the sound was getting louder, I determined it was coming in the direction of Joel's apartment. I looked around one last time and retraced my steps, closing the door quietly behind me as I left. Rather than wait for the elevator, I made quick use of the staircase and exited the building, being deposited into the parking lot. On the way to my car, I had a moment of panic, thinking about fingerprints, until I realized my fingerprints should be there, having had dinner there a few nights ago. This realization spurred me on, race walking, but not running, to my car. I entered the car, started it, and drove out of the parking lot. About one block from the building, I pulled over when I saw flashing lights pull into the lot and park in front of building number three. They had shut the sirens down, as if to maintain an element of surprise. As the police officers entered the building, I pulled away.

My thoughts were a jumble as I drove to my apartment. Where could Joel have gone? Was he there when the visitors arrived? Had he stumbled upon them while they were inside? Was it connected to the search he was running for me? I couldn't help but think it was connected, since it seemed too coincidental. Damn! This could be my fault. I hoped he was safe and hiding. He was a resourceful guy. I sent him mental energy.

I tried to concentrate on my driving, not wanting to get pulled over for speeding, especially not in the mental condition in which I found myself. As I drove down the same highway I had taken to Joel's apartment, I saw flashing lights on the side of the road. As was required by local law, cars were moving out of the right lane to provide the responders with a safety buffer zone. I was driving in the middle of the three available lanes, so didn't make any move to change lanes. As I approached the flashing lights, I saw two police cars and a fire department ambulance parked on the shoulder. Against everything I knew to be the correct procedure, I slowed and moved into the right lane. I had a bad feeling and needed to see what I could see. Driving at a dangerously slow speed, I peered out the passenger's side window and saw the most disturbing of sights: the crumbled wreckage of an overturned black Toyota Celica lying in a ditch, with an occupied body bag lying next to it, as the EMTs approached with a gurney.

I forced my attention back to the road and resumed a normal driving speed as I fought to gain control of my emotions. What the hell had happened?!? I had a gut feeling that someone deliberately caused this and it might be linked to the apartment break-in. Therefore, I assumed it might also be connected to Joel's search on my behalf. I had caused the death of my friend! Shit, shit, shit, shit, shit! What the hell did he find and on which country's servers? Almost any country in the world could be responsible for this, although the Russians were at the top of my list, based on the language being spoken on that Homeland recording.

I needed help and there was only one person I could think of who had the qualifications.

My godfather.

LISA

"You bastard! I don't know who you are, but if I ever find out, you'd better hope I never find you," Lisa screamed into her phone.

A mechanized voice chuckled in response. "I am quaking in my shoes, Lisa." The voice paused before continuing. "I will assume that you spoke with your mother and she confirmed the scenario which I described."

Attempting to hold her fury in check, Lisa responded with a curt, "She did."

"Good." The caller took a deep breath before explaining, in what he or she thought to be a reasonable tone of voice, "You know, Lisa, you brought this upon yourself. If you weren't so stubborn and head-strong, we could have left your mother out of this."

"Typical. Blame the victim so you feel better about what you've done."

"Oh, I don't need to do anything to feel better about it. I do what needs to be done to complete the mission. Whatever it takes." This last was said in a tone of voice meant to project menace and, even with the mechanized alteration, did so successfully. It had the desired effect of causing Lisa to reconsider her aggressive tone, especially with her mother's life in the balance.

Forcing herself into a calmer state of being, Lisa closed her eyes and said, "So, what is *this*?"

"*This* is, as they say, above your paygrade. All you need to know is that we now expect your full cooperation."

"And that cooperation takes form how?" Lisa was not only curious, but knew the only hope of saving her mother was to cooperate, if only until she could get her hands on the antidote.

"That's a much better attitude, Ms. Jones. I'm glad to hear it."

When the voice didn't provide any further information, Lisa, losing patience, spat at the phone. "So? What is it, or do you want to engage in more games?"

"No games," a now more serious voice responded. "Your cooperation will take the form of acquiescence. When your phone rings and you hear the tones of your school theme song, you will force yourself to listen and succumb. You will tell yourself, consciously and subconsciously, not to fight the effects of your training. You will surrender to the training and complete the tasks given to you with no hesitation or doubts. Is that understood?"

Considering what she'd just been told, she did not immediately respond. Silence filled the invisible connection between phones. Finally, Lisa said, "I understand the concept you've outlined. What I don't understand is what you're talking about. Succumb to what? What training?"

"Perhaps someday you will be told the entire story, Lisa," the voice responded with what might have been empathy. "For now, that information is immaterial to the task that awaits."

"And what is that task?"

"Tonight, at 7:30, you will be in your office. Alone. Tell no one of our conversation. Make whatever excuses you might need to Stephan. Just be there alone," he emphasized again.

Lisa's thoughts were, "*They know about Stephan. They know who my parents are. What else could they know? Who the fuck is this guy?*" Aloud, she responded, "OK. Then what?"

"Your phone will ring, you will answer it and willingly give yourself over. When you answer the call, listen carefully, take calming deep breaths, and allow yourself to be carried away. Nothing else. It will be easy and painless, unlike the consequences your mother will face if you fail to cooperate."

The thought of her mother's painful impending death brought the rage back, and she tried to control it before what little remaining composure she had vanished. "Fine. When do I get the antidote?"

"When your task and the mission are complete. You'll know when that is. That is all for now. Thank you for your cooperation."

The call disconnected, leaving Lisa to stare at the phone in her hand as she shook with rage, feeling helpless and alone. Having determined that she had no choice, she put the phone down and sat heavily in her chair, saying to the room, "What the fuck is going on?"

SEEKING ADVICE

I walked up the footpath to the door of the well-kept brownstone row house and ascended the stairs. Confronted by the massive wooden door, I hesitated before either ringing the doorbell or raising the brass door knocker. I hadn't called ahead, as was my custom. Based on the reason for my visit, something told me it would be best to show up unannounced. Overcoming my hesitancy, I pushed the button and listened to the tones echo through the door. As I waited, I took in my surroundings. Well-maintained homes, nicely manicured lawns and large trees. My godfather had done well for himself. I focused my attention on the home in front of me as I continued to wait. I noticed discreetly placed cameras on two sides of the exterior walls, covering the front stoop on which I waited. Turning, I looked at the large tree in the front yard. It took concentration, but I could discern at least two camouflaged cameras, each aimed in a different direction of the sidewalk and street. I guess old habits die hard. More likely was that he was much more in tune with how to protect himself and his property than I would ever be. I turned my attention back to the door just as it opened.

"Well, look at this. An unannounced visit by my godson." A smile spread across his face as he took a step back, allowing me to enter, and embraced me in a powerful hug. He may have been retired, but from the hug, it was clear that he still worked out on a regular basis. Releasing the embrace, he took a step back and gave me the once over, as if I were a racehorse and he was deciding whether to buy. Having completed his assessment, he said, "You look good, Stephan, although it looks as if you could use some sleep."

"Perceptive as always, Colonel."

"Not Colonel any more. Nowadays, it's plain old Dan."

"I don't think I'll ever be able to do that, sir."

"And enough with the formality."

He moved into the house and beckoned me to follow, which I did, noticing the dark wood tones in the hallway on our way to the kitchen. I was struck by the difference between this house and the one in which I had grown up. My father was a lifelong Sergeant and lived with my mother in a humble, but sufficient bungalow, near to the base. Somehow, my father had been befriended by an up-and-coming officer, one with whom he got along and shared many interests. They had become so close that my parents asked him to be my godfather and to look out for me if anything happened to them, which, ultimately, happened, leaving me an orphan. True to his word, Dan Fowler kept an eye on me and my career through the years. I knew, in the way one knows things they don't actually "know," that my godfather was involved in some aspect of the military intelligence community, which is why I was now following him into his kitchen to disclose possibly incriminating information. I wasn't comfortable doing so, but, to my mind, had no viable alternatives.

Once in the kitchen, Dan motioned for me to take a seat at the table while he moved to the ever-present coffee maker located on his counter. Without asking, he poured each of us a cup and joined me at the table, the steam rising and the aroma captivating me.

"So, to what do I owe this surprise visit?"

I lifted the cup to my lips, blew into it, and took a satisfying sip. I was stalling and hoped that he hadn't picked up on my tactic. He said nothing and waited for me to respond, so I wasn't sure if my tactic had succeeded. Finally, I placed the cup on the table in front of me and said, "I seem to find myself in a...situation, and I could use some advice." I looked him in the eyes as I said, "I thought that, based on your professional experience in the intelligence community, you might be able to help." I watched and waited. To my surprise, he didn't come out with an outright denial.

"My professional experience in the intelligence community, you say." He sat back and let a smile visit his face as he met my eyes. "I guess none of us are ever as good at hiding or keeping secrets as we think." He took a sip from his cup before hastily adding, "Not that I'm admitting anything in that regard, mind you." Replacing his cup, he turned more serious. "So, what sort of 'situation' do you find yourself involved in?"

Knowing that this was my last chance to back out and not place another person in mortal danger, I didn't answer immediately. He watched me closely as my mind went through its machinations, the various scenarios playing out in my facial expressions.

"Before I tell you, I need you to know that what I'm about to tell you could place you in serious danger. Life-threatening danger. I want to know that you're OK with that, I mean, as OK as one can be with it, before I tell you anything. One person has already been killed because of this information, and I don't want to be responsible for any more deaths."

I could see an emotion register on his features for the briefest of instances, but there was no way for me to know what that emotion was. Had the fact of a death made this more real for him and not just an imagining of his godson, whom he had decided to hear out because of their relationship? I waited.

"Life-threatening danger. Hmm. It's been a long time since I've been placed in life-threatening danger." He took another sip of coffee and continued. "Stephan, I can't tell you what my job was, but I can tell you that life-threatening danger was part of my job description."

He watched me for a reaction. I merely nodded my head.

"As a matter of fact, a life-threatening situation may just be what I need at the moment. Retirement ain't all that it's cracked up to be." This last was said with evident genuine regret at the decision the military had forced him to make.

Once I was certain he understood the stakes, I made my decision and launched into a lengthy and detailed explanation for the reason behind my appearance on his doorstep. He listened without interruption, taking in all that I said as if it were a debriefing and I his asset. When I had completed my tale, he fetched me a glass of water, placed it in front of me and re-took his seat as I drained the glass.

"So, what do you think?" I implored.

"It's quite a lot to take in, Stephan. I believe, based on the information as you've described it, that your conclusion is the only logical one you could have possibly reached."

For some reason, hearing *those* words come from *this* man made me feel immeasurably better.

"So, what do I do?"

It appeared to me that my godfather was becoming fidgety, although he worked hard to keep it under control and unnoticed. Finally, he said, "For the time being, do nothing, except watch your back. I agree that the death of your friend is just a little too coincidental to be dismissed. In the meantime, I still have some contacts in the intelligence arena. Let me make some discreet inquiries and see what I can find out. I'll get back to you as soon as I can."

He stood and I could tell by his bearing that the meeting was over and I was being dismissed. I rose and followed him to the door, where he turned, held out his hand and pulled me in for a bro hug, whispering in my ear, "Be careful." We disengaged, and he nodded at me as he opened the door, depositing me on his front stoop.

•   •   •

On my drive home, I replayed the meeting in my mind, watching it in my head as if watching a movie. I began with my approach to the house and finished with my exit and reappearance on the stoop. The unofficial revelation of my godfather's professional life did not overly surprise me. After all, it was my reason for confiding in him. It pleased me that his conclusion matched mine, but there was something tickling the back of my mind. Something I couldn't quite put to words, but was, nevertheless, present. He had agreed to make, as he put it, discreet inquiries. I assumed he meant to keep it discreet in an effort to avoid my court-martial and both of our violent deaths. Or was I making this out to be more than it actually was?

He seemed concerned, but not, "Oh My God, don't even leave this house!" concerned. Maybe he was just used to these kinds of situations. As he said, life-threatening danger had been part of his job description. I convinced myself that must be it. Just the difference between a professional and an amateur. I had always trusted him, unquestioningly. He had given me no reason to doubt either his ability or sincerity. Yet, there was still this unformed, unnamed, thing gnawing at the back of my consciousness. I decided to let it ride and work itself out in time. In the meantime, being careful seemed like a great idea, if I only had an idea how to go about doing so.

•   •   •

In my car and preparing to head home, I called Lisa. It seemed like ages since we'd spoken and eons since we'd been together. Isn't the perception of time an odd thing? I dialed her number and put the call on my car's speaker. The ringing was persistent but unanswered. Disappointed, I disconnected and pulled away from the curb, glancing back at the house before entering traffic. I may have been mistaken, but I thought I glimpsed my godfather moving away from the window. I told myself it was nothing and concentrated on my driving, not wanting to end up like my late friend Joel. Even so, I redialed Lisa, once again listening to the unanswered ringing. I glanced at the time and noted that it was usually a time she was available. So, being the persistent nag that I can be when I decide to dig in my heals, I redialed yet again, and again. Finally, she answered. She sounded exasperated, apparently with me, instead of being her usual calm and loving self.

"Stephan, do you think you've called enough in the last ten minutes? I can't really talk."

Wow! This was not the person to whom I was used to speaking.

"Lisa? Is that you?"

"Who else could it be answering my phone?"

Definitely perturbed.

"Well, it certainly sounds like your voice, but it definitely doesn't sound like you using it. What's up? Are you OK?"

I could hear her take a deep breath and, I thought, hold back a sob. I waited, interjecting nothing into the silence.

"I'm sorry. I just have a lot going on right now and I'm really stressed out."

"Want me to come over? We can release some stress together."

That actually elicited a giggle, which was, to my mind, a good sign.

"I wish we could, but I have to head back to the lab. A special project I can't really talk about."

"Oh. I thought you'd be getting some well-deserved down time. No rest for the wicked, I guess."

"None." She hesitated and started to say something, but stopped. Instead, she said, "Listen, I may be out of touch for a few days or so. I'll call you as soon as I can. OK?"

What could I say, other than, "OK. I'll talk to you soon. Love you."

"Love you too."

The call disconnected, and I was left with nothing other than dead air and my very confused thoughts.

LISA

Lisa let the phone slip from her hand onto the couch cushion, making no attempt to save it. She punched the pillow sitting innocently next to her as she repeated, "Shit, shit, shit, shit, shit," in time with her punches. Suddenly ending her barrage, she let herself cry. Long, hard, emotional sobs, which went on and on, unabated, until she had no tears left. The tears shed had been born of both rage and frustration at her unknown tormentor and had served the purpose of allowing her to rid herself of unwanted emotion. Purged of the rage and frustration, she hoped she could follow the instructions given to her and devote herself to the mysterious training to save her mother. Once that had been accomplished, she would confide in Stephan and together they would hunt down the mysterious voice behind whatever this mission turned out to be. At least, that's what she forced herself to believe. For the time being, she was determined to not only save her mother, but protect Stephan from a similar fate. Resigned, she retrieved her phone from where it had fallen, cleaned her face, and headed for the lab.

•   •   •

Seated at her desk at the prescribed time, Lisa waited impatiently for the call she knew would be forthcoming. She stared at the phone, willing it to ring and get this ordeal over with. As she waited, she couldn't help but think, *"What fucking training was he talking about?"* Try as she had since she'd heard about it, she could not conjure any image that recalled any "training" which could possibly be to what the caller was referring. She had gone through potty training, as had every other child she'd known. There had been musical instrument (piano) training. Even dance (ballet) training. But, none of that was going to be recalled with the upcoming call, unless this mysterious *mission* required her to perform a jete on her way to the bathroom, where she would pee while playing a piano strategically placed near the toilet. Highly unlikely.

At 7:30, she checked the time and increased the intensity of her staring, hoping that by sheer will the call would come through. The time continued to tick, moving forward at a snail's pace. At 7:35, she thought she'd burst unless the phone rang. At 7:40, she could no longer sit and wait, instead pacing back and forth in front of her desk. She never took her eyes from the phone, utilizing the spotting technique learned those many years ago at ballet while changing directions. Finally, at 7:44, the phone rang, and she ran to connect the call.

"I apologize for my tardiness, Ms. Jones," said the mechanized voice, "but there were some pressing matters that required my attention. Are you ready to proceed?"

Through gritted teeth, her jawbones aching, she said, "Yes," as she took her seat.

"Excellent. I suppose I don't need to remind you what is riding on your ability to succumb to your training."

"No, you don't," she responded, the hatred seething from her every pore. "Let's get on with it already."

"Excellent." After a brief pause, during which Lisa could hear what sounded like papers shuffling, the caller continued. "You will hear the theme song for your old prep school. Sit back, close your eyes, and breath slowly and deeply, as if meditating. Clear your mind and just listen. I will be able to determine your state of consciousness. Once I am satisfied, you will receive your instructions. Ready?"

"Yes."

With no further discussion, the tones of *La Voltaire et La Franklein* emanated from the tiny speaker imbedded in her phone. She sat back, closed her eyes, and made a monumental effort to relax. Trying that hard to relax could only result in the opposite effect, much like trying not to run your tongue over that slight toothache once you'd inadvertently done so. Try as she might, she only succeeded in making herself more anxious about her inability to let herself go.

"Damn it!" she shouted. "Relaxing shouldn't be so hard to do!"

"Perhaps, Ms. Jones, you should try thinking about something pleasant instead of focusing so intently on relaxing," came the mechanized advice of her persecutor.

As the notes of her school theme song continued to fill the surrounding space, she couldn't help but think aloud, "Something pleasant, hmm. Perhaps wringing your neck."

"If that would work to calm you, please feel free to envision such a wringing." The smugness of the answer was almost tangible.

Whispering, "Asshole," to herself, she again closed her eyes and leaned back in her chair, willing her body to release the tightness which had taken hold of her muscles. She conjured an image of Stephan and recalled a weeklong trip they had made to a pristine Caribbean beach. She recalled lying in a comfortable lounge chair nestled into the fine white sand while listening to the waves as they gently landed on shore. She remembered reaching for Stephan's hand as he matched her position in a lounge chair of his own, set inches away from hers. As their hands touched in her mind, she had, without realizing it, completely relaxed and succumbed to the hidden sounds embedded in *La Voltaire et La Franklein.*

"Very good, Lisa," said a gentle version of the automated voice. "Please count backwards from one hundred for me."

With no discussion or retort of any kind, Lisa immediately complied as her caller listened intently to the intonation of her voice and assessed her condition. At the count of seventy, the voice said, "You may stop counting now, Lisa. I am very proud of you. Everyone is proud of you and what you've accomplished. Now, listen very carefully to my instructions. Once I have disconnected from this call, you will immediately follow those instructions to the letter and, when your work has been completed, you will return home, go to bed, and awaken refreshed and with no memory of this evening other than a pleasant night spent at home. Do you understand?"

Dreamily she responded, "Yes."

"Excellent," an obviously pleased voice responded. After a momentary pause, during which Lisa could hear a faint shuffling of papers, the voice began its Russian language recitation of instructions, the speaker now confident she would follow them precisely.

In her chair, Lisa listened intently with her eyes closed, the rapid side-to-side movement of her eyeballs vivid against the skin of her eyelids, blissfully unaware of the task on which she was about to embark.

DAN FOWLER'S HOUSE

As soon as Stephan had left the walkway to the house, Dan briskly turned and went up the stairs to his office, taking them two at a time. Once there, he sat, unlocked a desk drawer, and removed a yellow legal pad on which were hand-written notes. As had become his habit, he kept notes of his meetings with Bob Ferguson, jotting down not only facts, but ideas, recollections, and perceptions. He had decided to use the written word, on paper, as a measure of security, knowing how easily vulture-like technicians could access almost any computer and strip its contents to the bone. He needed to look no further than Stephan's friend, Joel, to see what even a non-professional could accomplish with readily available tools and software. His legal pad was safer, to his mind, especially when coupled with the loaded Colt revolver also kept in the same desk drawer.

He placed the pad on his desk and flipped through its pages. In this instance, it wasn't what he had written, but rather what was missing that was of interest to him. During his most recent meeting with his boss, at which he had been given a new assignment, he was advised that a computer breach had been detected. It was attempting not only to break into the computer system of every U.S. intelligence agency, but had been tracked to computer systems of other world powers. The source of the breach, while being well hidden, had ultimately been traced by investigators to an apartment outside of Washington, D.C., in a suburb located in Virginia. The lease to the apartment in question was in the name of a member of the United States Army who happened to work at the United States Army Intelligence and Security Command Center. Homeland Security was worried that other countries being similarly attacked would trace the problem to Corporal Joel Clark, placing blame for the computer breach squarely on the shoulders of the U.S. government. While everybody with any security clearance knew the security breaches were not government sanctioned operations, behind the closed doors of various executive suites the determination was made to stop the attacks, confiscate the computers, and send a clear message to the world's intelligence agencies that the United States was not behind this and the issue had been firmly and finally dealt with. That was Dan Fowler's mission, and he had carried it out swiftly and with precision. At no point in his briefing had the fact of Corporal Clark's friendship with his godson come up, and it was this omission that Dan had found glaring. For a moment Dan let himself believe that, just maybe, Director Ferguson had not known of the connection, but, upon further mental review, knowing how thorough Homeland was, knew this to be a fantasy of the highest order.

Thinking back to a prior conversation with Ferguson, Dan took a trip back in time via yellow pad pages until he came to the notes from his initial meeting. He recollected a conversation about why his old protégé had turned to him for a job and was certain he had made a notation. Flipping through pages, he found himself in the correct timeframe. He slowed and more carefully perused the pages until he came upon the passage for which he had been searching:

I asked, basically, why me Bob? He said he could use an assistant and, being familiar with my skill-set, thought I'd be perfect. I asked about which particular skill-set he meant and he said the part that respects confidentiality and puts our country before personal gain or relationships.

There it was in his own handwriting: *the part that puts our country before personal gain or relationships.*

"Son of a bitch. The bastard knew something at our first meeting. Maybe I trained him a little too well."

He let the pages of the pad fall into place as he leaned back in his chair and contemplated his situation. Something was going on and he was coming to the realization that he hadn't been read into the entire operation. Would he be put into the position of having to choose between his country or protecting his godson? If so, would he do as he always had, or would he break new ground in his personal code of conduct?

"Well, shit," was all he could think to say as he left his office and retreated down the stairs to his bar, ready to pour himself a tall, stiff drink.

•   •   •

At the headquarters of Homeland Security the following day, Dan Fowler had to wait until 11:00 a.m. for an audience with his boss. Once admitted to the Director's office, he took a seat and, as was his habit, engaged in no small talk before getting to business.

"I had an interesting visit from my godson yesterday."

This got Bob Ferguson's attention, as Dan had hoped. Ferguson looked up from the paperwork at which he'd been staring, raised an eyebrow, and said, "Really? Pray tell."

"He had an interesting story about an intercepted recording that was assigned to him for investigation. That recording came from Homeland Security, but you knew that already."

Fowler watched his boss for any telltale sign of acknowledgment, but received none. Instead, Ferguson simply said, "Go on."

"He told a tale of discovering a hidden signal in an intercepted recording, despite being instructed by his Commanding Officer to let it go. During his personal investigation, he happened upon an identical signal hidden in what he thought was a totally unrelated source, one that he had personally recorded at, of all places, The Franklin School reunion."

Still no outward reaction from the Director, who merely nodded and said, "Hmm. That is interesting."

"It turns out that Stephan had a friend, a certain Corporal Joel Clark, with whom he worked. This Corporal Clark had a vast computer hobby and had agreed to assist my godson in attempting to piece together the mystery of the hidden sounds. Now, Stephan had no idea whether his friend's attempts were successful, because, before they could meet to discuss it, Corporal Clark had a fatal car accident."

"Yes, that was tragic, wasn't it?" asked Ferguson, making a futile attempt to hide the smirk fighting to make an appearance on his face.

Fowler leaned forward and, in a quiet, menacing tone, said, "Bob, I know I don't have the complete picture. Hell, I probably only have a small fraction of the picture. But I need to know what the fuck is going on. How much danger is Stephan in?" He leaned back and waited for a response.

Instead, Ferguson pushed his chair back from his desk, got up, and came around, headed for his office door, and said, as he passed Fowler, "Let's go for a ride in that very comfy and secure limo, shall we?"

Instantly, Fowler bounded out of his seat and followed his boss, hoping for a measure of clarity.

•   •   •

The occupants were still getting settled and comfortable as the limousine pulled out of the underground garage. This time Fowler accepted the offered bottle of water, immediately cracking open the seal and gulping half the bottle. Until that very moment, he hadn't realized just how thirsty he was. Drinking helped to fill the silence in the car, as neither party spoke until well clear of the building from which they had just emerged.

"If I had told you about Stephan's connection to Corporal Clark, would it have made any difference in whether you carried out your mission?"

Fowler, not having expected this as an opening, blinked and said, "I suppose not."

"That's what I thought. So, from a practical standpoint, whether you had, or didn't have, that information was immaterial. That's why I didn't tell you. It made no difference. The fact of the matter is that Corporal Clark's actions posed a threat which needed to be eliminated."

Fowler had no retort to this. As a matter of fact, he completely agreed, so remained silent.

Continuing, Ferguson said, "In fact, your relationship with Sergeant Beck is the one thing that kept him, and, so far, is keeping him out of harm's way." Pausing, he reconsidered. "Well, that may not actually be accurate. It was a factor in keeping him out of harm's way. The other factor is that he may be of use to us. Soon."

"Of use, how?"

Director Ferguson leaned back and sighed. "For that, you will need to know what the big picture is. I hope my initial assessment of your abilities and general outlook will prove my faith in you was not misplaced."

Knowing he could now be placing his life in jeopardy, Fowler said, "I take it you're referring to putting our country before personal considerations, which has always been my inclination. I suppose we'll find out once I hear your story."

"I suppose we will, Dan." Nodding his head in agreement, he repeated, "I suppose we will."

•　　•　　•

"Several years ago, an American operative had the good fortune of coming across a cache of documents relating to various Russian operations. Somebody gave them a cursory review and shoved them into a drawer, not deeming anything he'd read worthy of immediate attention. I have no idea how many other people read any of the documents and came to the same conclusion, but the documents remained hidden and forgotten. I can only assume the reason for such inaction was that all the documentation dealt with operations that had been terminated by the Russians. The thinking must have been that, if they were no longer active, they were no longer of interest."

Fowler nodded his head and said, "Makes sense. Especially with the ever present budgetary concerns that seem to control what gets attention and what doesn't."

"Exactly. In any event, those documents were moved around and stored, where they lay dormant and forgotten for years."

"Until you found them."

"Until I found them," Ferguson echoed. He paused to drink from his water bottle before continuing. "As you said, I found the documents and, without any specific interest in them, started flipping through the pages. I completely understood why nobody ever did anything with them. It shocked me they even existed. As I was about to toss them aside, I noticed one thing of interest. A name." He paused and stared at Fowler, who stared back, unmoving and mute, which prompted Ferguson to continue.

"Pushkin."

Fowler shook his head and repeated, "Pushkin." He took a drink from his water bottle and said, "That bastard is the proverbial bad penny. He just keeps turning up. Why won't he just die, already?" he asked rhetorically.

Ferguson chuckled and continued. "He is, and has definitely been, a constant pain in our asses. Anyway, it was seeing his name that made me go back to those documents and pay them more attention. Do you remember that huge facility in the middle of nowhere that we had such a hard time getting information on?"

"Of course. Did the documents deal with that facility?" His interest was now piqued.

"They did. And more. It turns out the facility housed fake American towns where Russian deep cover spies lived, worked, and were schooled in being 'Americanized.' They were totally immersed in American culture and weren't even allowed to speak Russian. Our friend Pushkin was in charge of the entire operation. His second in command is the now Russian Ambassador to the United States."

"Unbelievable."

"Oh, it gets even more so. During the détente years, with US/Russian relations becoming more relaxed, the Russians slipped those spies into the country with apparent ease, where they lived, worked, and propagated, just like the rest of the unaware U.S. citizenry. Eventually, the old guard lost power and, with the rise of Gorbachev and the supposed end of the Cold War, the program was abandoned and the deep cover spies never activated."

"That's a very interesting history lesson, and the fact that Pushkin and his pal Ovechkin were involved gives it some personal meaning, but what does it have to do with anything?"

"Well, as I said, those deep cover spies lived and propagated in the US. Their children, as your godson would have been had he not been rescued, were educated at schools set up by Pushkin and Ovechkin."

"The Franklin Schools."

"Exactly. The Franklin Schools. What I learned about the Franklin Schools and their curriculum was that the real reason behind the school's existence was to have a platform to indoctrinate the offspring of the deep cover spies. Deep cover spies 2.0, if you will. The school subjected the children to intense programming using drugs and audio triggers, enabling them to be activated remotely when necessary. With the program having been ended, these unknowing spies remained dormant and just went on with their lives as US citizens, having no idea about their parents or their own true potential."

Ferguson again leaned back and relaxed, drinking deeply from his water bottle. The two agents sat silently, each deep in his own thoughts. Finally, the lightbulb went on in Fowler's mind. He leaned forward and looked up at his boss with a look of incredulity etched on his face.

"You activated the kids."

"I did," was the smug reply.

"To do what?"

With renewed fervor in his voice, Ferguson said, "To help us get this country back on track and rid ourselves of all these namby-pamby sell-out politicians. Enough is enough, don't you agree?"

Knowing full well that his life now hung in the balance, and believing in the cause having been voiced by his former protégé, he sincerely replied, "I do."

Ferguson let himself relax and said, "I thought you might. That's why I brought you aboard."

In response, a newly interested Fowler asked, "So, how are these kids going to do that?"

Ferguson smiled and replied, "Brilliantly."

HOW'S LISA?

It took Lisa more than just the one night at the lab to fulfill her obligation to what she had come to think of as "The Voice." After the second grueling all-nighter, she returned home, left a message on her bosses' phone stating that she wouldn't be coming in that day, and went right to bed. When she finally awoke around 2:00 p.m., she felt rested and relaxed, just as she had been instructed. She thought she remembered spending a nice evening at home, but something didn't quite feel right to her. If that had been the case, why hadn't she awoken in the morning and gone to work? That once familiar strange feeling was back, and it was disconcerting. It brought back memories of the feelings she'd had not that long ago, just around the time of her great scientific breakthrough. As she sat at her dining room table drinking coffee, she continued to wonder why she hadn't gone to work. She concentrated and was able to recall a conversation about a package her mother had received and that was enough to jolt her out of her programmed stupor.

"Fuck! That bastard almost had me forgetting." No longer relaxed, she went to her computer, hoping beyond hope to find a mysterious email containing the key to curing her mother's as yet dormant illness. Finding no such correspondence, she slammed her fist on the table and shouted at the computer, "Come on, you bastard! I did my part, I think. Give me the cure!"

As if in answer to her ranting, the chime of an incoming email caught her attention. Checking the sender information, she saw it had been blocked, which, in this instance, gave her hope. Opening it, she read:

"Ms. Jones, although I know that you have no actual recollection of what you've done, I would like you to know that your work over the last two nights has been exemplary. I'm certain that you are anxious to obtain the antidote to your mother's condition, and I can assure you that the time for that is rapidly approaching. One more step remains to be accomplished for the completion of our mission. You will be receiving an invitation to a very special event being given in Washington, D.C. in a few days. With the invitation, you will find a data stick. Just before leaving for the event, insert the stick into your computer and listen to your final set of instructions. Do not attend the affair without listening to the audio file. The results of doing so would prove fatal to your mother. Once the evening has been completed, the information you require will be provided."

As soon as she had finished reading, the email disappeared as a video of a flame appeared on the screen, accompanied by the sound of a raging fire. She searched her email trash bin, the computer's general trash bin, and anyplace else she thought it might have gone.

"Couldn't I have at least gotten a *Mission Impossible* style five-second warning?" she said to her monitor, not expecting a reply, but not certain one would not be forthcoming. When she was greeted with silence, she resigned herself to what appeared to be her fate: awaiting further instructions.

"I can't wait to get my hands on this asshole."

Realizing how hungry she was, and having no memory of the last time she had eaten, she left the computer and headed for the kitchen when her cell phone awakened from its slumber. Glad not to hear the tones of La Voltaire et La Franklein, which she hoped never to hear again, she glanced at caller ID, surprised to see Jennifer's name displayed, although it occurred to her it might not actually be Jennifer. It had been quite some time since they'd been in touch outside of the office and she still missed the companionship. Smiling, she answered the call as she made her way to the refrigerator.

"Hey, Jen. What's up?"

"Hi Lisa. I was hoping you could tell me. I heard you'd called in sick and wanted to check on you."

Lisa foraged through her opened refrigerator, as she said, "Thanks for checking, Jen. It's nothing, really. I just needed a little time off. Getting those papers ready for peer review has taken a toll." Amazed, she thought to herself, "*The lies just flow so easily.*"

"Oh yeah. I'd forgotten about that," replied Jennifer, having not forgotten about that for an instant. "You must be exhausted."

"I am. How are you?"

"I'm good. Starting to work on some other things, now that you've beaten us all to the punch for the big prize."

"Oh, Jen. You know, in our line of work there's always a new 'next big prize.' My work was just a steppingstone to whatever comes next."

"You're right, of course. I'm just feeling sorry for myself. A few more days of wallowing should do it," she laughed.

Glad to hear her friend's laughter, she joined in as she replied, "Enjoy it while you can."

"Will do," was the jovial response. "Get some rest. Let's get together soon."

"I'd like that. Thanks. See you soon."

The conversation helped buoy Lisa's emotional well-being, for reasons she couldn't begin to fathom. Maybe it was the feeling of normalcy it brought, after the mysterious calls from the mechanized voice and all those calls brought with them. Feeling better, she gathered ingredients and threw together what she thought was a damn good omelet.

•   •   •

Jennifer disconnected the call and sat alone in her office. She stared out her window as she wondered what Lisa had really been up to. She knew Lisa had been in contact with the same mysterious voice as she had, although she had no idea to what end. It amazed Jennifer that she could so easily play the role of a good friend on the one hand and the Judas on the other. She liked to think that the dual roles bothered her, but in those rare moments of true self-honesty, realized that reality was different. It didn't bother at her at all, which in itself should have bothered her, but again, did not. Turning back to the work waiting on her computer, she thought, "*You know, I'd make a really excellent spy, just like in those old Cold War novels.*" The thought brought a genuine smile to her face.

BACK AT THE HOMELAND LIMOUSINE

Fowler wasn't sure if Ferguson was speaking about the kid's abilities or his own plan, so, rather than say anything, merely raised an eyebrow and said, "How so?"

"There's a company called United Genetics Research. They are a cutting edge lab doing genetic/DNA research. It just so happens that a couple of the spy kids work there and are the leading researchers. I set up a covert company and provided funding to expedite the research. Having read the records of these two particular Franklin graduates, I knew that the chances of success were high. Especially when it came to one of them."

He paused as he assessed what he was about to say, trying to gauge the reaction before actually providing the information. Inwardly having made a decision, he continued.

"You may be familiar with one name. Lisa Jones."

Fowler considered the name for a moment before understanding registered on his face. "Stephan's girlfriend?"

"The same."

Silence ensued as Fowler looked out his window and mulled over the implications. After a minute, he turned back to his boss.

"So, you made certain that Stephan was assigned the intercepted message, just on the off chance that somebody connected the dots."

Ferguson nodded, knowing that Fowler still had more to say.

"Why not bury the message? For that matter, why was the message in Russian? If you were the one doing the activation, why not your native language?"

"The programming had been done in Russian, a language the kids didn't, and don't, even know they understood. I masked the message as best

I could, but knowing our own capabilities, had a feeling that it would be flagged. Had I buried it, suspicions might have been aroused, and I couldn't risk it."

"So, knowing Stephan's background, his relationship with Lisa, who was a pawn of yours, and Stephan's relationship to me, you made certain to keep the loop as closed as possible."

"Under the circumstances, yes. I thought it would be prudent."

"So, what did Lisa do?"

"She created a targeted disease that will affect only the specific person for whom it had been designed. It's absolutely harmless to anybody else. It's a natural form of assassination. Unlike a gunshot, it is undetectable, works over time rather than instantly, will not draw undue attention, and will not fail. Nobody will ever know it was anything other than a natural occurrence."

Something occurred to Fowler, and he asked, "So, what about Lisa? Is her part in this done?"

Surprised by what he deemed to be apprehension, Ferguson said, "Dan, your concern for Lisa is, I must say, somewhat unexpected."

"I'm thinking more about Stephan. He really loves her."

"In any operation, there are casualties. As someone taught me many years ago, a good plan has a fall-guy. Or in this case, a fall-girl." Ferguson observed Fowler's reaction before asking, "Is that going to be a problem?"

Without hesitation, Fowler answered, "Of course not. You learned well, padawan."

Taken completely off guard by the sudden joking cultural reference, Ferguson actually guffawed. When finished, he wiped the tears from his eyes and said, "Dan, I didn't think you had it in you. I now truly believe that anything is possible."

A NEW ASSIGNMENT FOR STEPHAN

I went to work having not yet heard from my godfather. After what had happened to Joel, my nerves were on edge and my head on a swivel. Not a good way to live, but here I was. When I got to my cubicle, I couldn't help but notice his absence. People had left mementos on his desk, as well as flowers and notes. I expected his head to appear on his pretend hydraulic lift and waited for it. When I was left disappointed, I found tears escaping my eyes and rolling down my cheek. How the hell was I supposed to get any work done, especially while bursting with guilt over his fate?

I took my seat and opened my secure email, expecting to find new intercepted messages and assignments. Something to take my mind off Joel's absence and assuage some of the guilt, at least temporarily. Instead, I found a brief and, I would say, curt, summons from my commanding officer. I couldn't help but think, *"Oh shit, now what? Are they going to lead me away in handcuffs?"*

I made my way to his office, doing my best to avoid eye contact with anybody else, thinking that everybody must know who's really to blame for Joel's death. The guilt was eating me up. When I arrived, the door was closed and his receptionist asked me to have a seat. I did. I couldn't help but fidget and felt eyes boring into me, even if I couldn't see the heads in which they lived. I was convinced that "they" all knew, and this was part of my self-inflicted punishment. At last, I heard my name called and was ushered into the CO's office. When the door closed behind me, I imagined the clicking sound as that of a cell door being slid into place.

I approached the desk at which sat my commanding officer, Colonel Kreuzer, the son of German immigrants and a first rate linguist in his own right. We had always gotten along, as well as a Sergeant and his CO could be deemed to "get along." I stood at attention, waiting to be recognized, but was ignored for at least a full minute, which seemed much longer while standing at full attention and trying to control the amount of sweat leaking from my armpits. Finally, he looked up from the papers at which he had been staring, looked at me, and scowled. He stared at me with the scowl imprinted onto his features and, after some time, returned my salute, but did not invite me to sit. In my head, I heard myself saying, *"Oh shit, oh shit, oh shit."*

"Sergeant, Beck. I believe I had instructed you to cease working on that Russian intercept we had previously discussed."

"Uh oh, here it comes," I thought. In answer I merely said, in as loud and authoritative a voice as I could muster, "Yes, sir."

"And, based on your log-in records and reports, it appears that you had done so."

Not having been asked a question, and understanding the nuance in the statement, I stood my ground in silence.

"And yet, I have before me transfer orders for you. It seems that your presence has been requested at Homeland Security for a special assignment."

The surprise evident on my face, I could only respond by saying, "Homeland wants me for an assignment?"

"So, you have not contacted anybody at Homeland about the recording or anything else?" It sounded as if he had suspicions.

"No, sir. I have not."

"And you have not been contacted by anybody at Homeland?"

"No, sir. I have not."

"Are you familiar with a Director Robert Ferguson?"

The name rang a faint bell, so I searched my memory tapes before answering. "The name sounds a little familiar, sir." I paused to delve further into my memory banks. "I believe many years ago he worked with someone with whom I am acquainted. But I can assure you that I have not seen nor heard from him in many years."

"Um hm. Well, it appears this Director Ferguson, who just coincidentally happens to be the person who sent that intercepted message on which you were working, has personally requested your assistance in, and I'm quoting here, 'A highly classified matter of imminent national security.'" He looked up from his papers as his eyes attempted to bore holes into my skull. "I was not aware, Sergeant, that you had such clearance."

"No, sir. Neither was I." *What the hell was going on?*

"OK, Beck. I don't know what's going on here, but my hands are tied. I'm not in a position to deny this transfer. I just hope that you haven't done anything that's going to come back and bite either of us in the ass, and when I say *us*, I mean *me*." He searched me for any telltale signs of deceit. I hoped I had successfully hidden the guilt I was feeling over having taken that recording and Joel's death. I must have satisfied any lingering suspicions, since he handed me my orders and brusquely said, "Dismissed."

I snapped a brisk salute, executed a flawless about face, and marched out of his office, thinking, "*This could only be because my godfather talked to him. What am I getting into?*"

•   •   •

I arrived at Homeland Security headquarters, checked in, and was led to the wing which housed Director Robert Ferguson. I hadn't seen him in probably twenty or more years, so had no idea what to expect. When I appeared in front of his secretary, she greeted me in a friendly manner, as if my standing in front of her was a daily occurrence.

"Sargent Beck. Nice to meet you. Director Ferguson is tied up in a meeting down the hall. He asked that I show you into his office so you don't have to wait out here."

Rising from her chair, she beckoned me to follow, which I did. At the entry to the Director's office, she opened the door, stood aside and motioned for me to proceed, which I also did.

"Please make yourself comfortable. There's a pitcher of ice water and glasses on the table. Please help yourself."

Before I could turn around and thank her, the door clicked shut. I wondered whether it was locked from the outside, but didn't dare test it, mostly because I didn't want my fears to be confirmed, but also because I didn't want anybody outside of the door noticing the knob twisting and nobody emerging, which, in this particular location, could be taken as a sign of guilt, or worse.

I walked to the table, poured myself a glass of water and, glass in hand, surveyed the room. I was too nervous to just sit and wait, so I walked around, looking at the typical mementos found in upper echelon offices: pictures with high-ranking politicians, old military pictures, golf course pictures with high-ranking military personnel, etc. What I didn't find was anything of a personal nature. No pictures of a wife, kids, grandkids. Some people made work their life and, apparently, Director Ferguson was one of those people. I made my way to his desk and sat in one of the two chairs, which were waiting for someone to use them. As I sat there, not wanting to be too conspicuous, I looked at the desk and at the credenza behind it. As expected, there was not much of interest to be seen on either, since, I was certain, the Director dealt with classified matters and wouldn't leave documents of any import lying around for any visitor to see. What I did see, pushed into a cubby of the credenza, but still visible to one who knew what it looked like, and which probably meant nothing to anybody other than another sound geek, was a Roland Voice Transformer model VT4. I'd read about them, and seen pictures, but hadn't yet been up close and personal with one. Supposedly, it was top of the line equipment, capable of changing a voice so that even people closest to the user wouldn't recognize to whom they were speaking. Unable to control myself, I began to rise from my seat, thinking I'd inspect it a little closer, when the office entry door opened. Hearing it, I shifted my focus and turned towards the door, hoping I hadn't been caught moving toward the credenza. Entering was Director Ferguson. He didn't look much different from the last time I'd seen him, more than two decades ago, although sporting a little more gray around the temples and more deeply etched facial worry lines. I placed my glass on the coaster which waited near the desk's edge and stepped forward to greet my temporary boss, or so I'd assumed.

Hand outstretched with a smile on his face, he approached and said, "Stephan, so good to see you. What's it been, twenty years or so?"

Accepting his hand and returning the smile, I said, "Director Ferguson, nice to see you too. And yes, it's been at least twenty years." I looked around at my surroundings and said, "I bet my godfather is more than a little jealous of this."

He laughed as he continued towards his desk, motioning for me to retake my seat. Once seated, he pressed a button on his desk phone and sat back expectantly. A moment later, his office door opened.

"You can ask him yourself," he said, still chuckling to himself.

I turned to find my godfather closing the door behind him and walking towards me. Stunned, I remained seated and silently staring, considering what this might mean, in light of the last conversation we'd had.

"I take it you're surprised to see me," he said as he took the seat next to me.

Shaking off my stupor, I said, "I am," as I looked from him to the Director and back.

As if reading my mind, he said, "Yes, when I said I still had some contacts, I was referring to Bob. Excuse me, Director Ferguson." He watched as I mentally digested the information. "For reasons that are, or should be, obvious, I couldn't tell you I worked for Homeland."

"You told him everything I told you?" I asked, hoping against hope that the answer would be negative.

"I did," was the reply.

When he saw the despondent look on my face, he held up his hand and said, "It's okay. We're here to see that you don't end up in the brig." He looked at his boss, our boss, for confirmation.

Director Ferguson nodded and said, "Provided, of course, that you can maintain a high level of confidentiality. I've raised your security clearance and have a few things for you to sign once you've decided to come aboard, at least temporarily."

I heard the thinly veiled threat and, rather than acknowledging it aloud, said only, "I understand."

The Director looked at his agent, nodded almost imperceptibly, and said, "Good."

•   •   •

The Director handed me a sheaf of papers, loosely bound in a binder bearing the Office of Homeland Security logo, and instructed me to review them. I did so, trying my best to get through the legal mumbo-jumbo without just asking to be arrested and sent to solitary confinement, which seemed like a lesser punishment. Understanding my predicament, and realizing that I really had no choice but to sign, I snatched the pen which awaited just within reach on the desk, searched for those pages requiring my signature, and quickly scribbled my name in the appropriate locations. Done, I closed the binder and handed it to Director Ferguson.

"Thank you, temporary agent," he said with a smile as he accepted the proffered documents.

I remained silent, waiting for the proverbial other shoe to drop. My wait was a short one.

"Stephan," my godfather turned to me and said, "the message you were working on is connected to the recording you made at the Franklin School reunion."

I stared at him as if he were speaking a language I'd never heard, since what he'd said remained incomprehensible to me. Recovering, I asked, "But, how is that possible?"

He turned to Director Ferguson, who continued.

"Stephan, what I'm about to tell you is so highly classified that only a handful of people in the world are privy to this information. It's also, I should warn you, pretty unbelievable, especially when viewed from today's vantage point. You are, I'm almost certain, not going to believe me, but I assure you, every word is true."

I looked at my godfather, who said, "He's right. You're going to think this was the plot of a novel, but it's all too true."

"*OK,*" I thought, "*let's find out what the hell is going on.*"

•   •   •

Director Ferguson took the lead.

"During the Cold War, in the 70s, the Soviets had a program which was intended to flood Americanized agents into the U.S. These agents had been living in fake American towns, instructed to speak only English, and lived and worked as if they were actually here. The plan was to bring them into the country, let them settle in, and then activate them once they had been accepted into society."

"That does sound like a movie or novel plot," I said. "How many of these agents were there?"

"Hundreds," was the reply.

"Multiple hundreds?" I asked.

"Yes."

"Holy shit," was what escaped by mouth before I could stop it.

"Exactly," said the Director.

"Did they actually implement the plan?" I had to know.

"They did," said Director Ferguson. "Not all the agents, but enough."

I looked at my godfather as I tried to understand the implications of what I was being told. He raised his eyebrows and nodded, seemingly knowing what was running through my mind.

"How?" was all I could think to ask.

"The Russians can be a very patient people. During a period of détente, we relaxed our oversight, and they were able to bring people in right under our noses."

His distaste for what he was saying was evident. It was as if he had to force himself into calmly making the statement. I could tell this was highly personal for him.

I asked, "So, if these agents had been here, how were they used? I've never heard anything about them."

My godfather, as if sensing how upset this made the Director, took over by saying, "That's because they never were used."

My surprise was obvious. "How can that be? It had to have been an enormous investment of time and money."

"Politics," was the short answer from my godfather. "Leaders change and the Cold War effectively ended. New leadership in Russia felt it would provoke hostilities if they'd been activated. So, the program was scrapped, and the agents left here to live their lives."

I got up to pour myself a glass of water, more to buy processing time than because I was thirsty. I returned to my seat, placed my glass on the coaster it had previously occupied, and went back to fetch the pitcher and glasses so that both the Director and my godfather could drink. After all, it was them doing all the talking.

As I retook my seat, I digested what I'd just heard. While the enterprise undertaken by the Soviets was huge in scope, it was amazing to me they had just let it go, effectively eliminating any return on what had to be an enormous investment. Someone over there must have known all of those quiet agents remained in the U.S. As my thoughts gained focus, I looked at Director Ferguson.

"Someone finally realized what they had here." I couched it as a statement, not a question.

Director Ferguson again took up the talking stick. "Someone finally did. Yes."

Still, something was missing. What did all of this have to do with the recording I took at the Franklin School reunion? I voiced my concerns.

"Something doesn't compute."

"Why do you say that?" he asked.

"Because all those people have been here for years and I can't see any connection with the Franklin School. How could they possibly be connected?"

"All those people lived here and had children." He said nothing else, letting that sink in and silently inviting me to work it out for myself. I remained silent, running it through it in my head. Finally, I looked at both of the men.

"The kids went to the Franklin School."

The talking stick was seemingly passed to my godfather, who said, "The Franklin School had been created by the Soviets before the end of the Cold War, specifically, and solely, for the children of the agents. There were schools set up all over the country."

"But, why?"

Somehow, the talking stick was returned to the Director, who continued, "I said the Soviets, the Russians, have patience. It turns out that the long game was for the kids to have the greater effect. Still, that program was also abandoned."

"Except that, whoever realized what had been left here, also realized the kids could still be an asset," I intuited. Thinking for a moment, I asked, "But how? Why the kids? Had they been taught by their parents?"

The Director continued, "The real reason behind the Franklin Schools was to program the kids to be agents, even if they didn't know it."

"Program?" I asked. "Program how?"

"By indoctrinating them at any early age through a series of drugs administered under the guise of vitamins. The drugs were actually meant to make it easier to control the children. A sort of high-tech hypnosis, if you will."

"Now I see what you meant. This whole thing is truly unbelievable."

My mind was swirling as I attempted to put this together. To my chagrin, the implications, on a personal level, finally hit home. I looked at each of the men, the look of horror giving away my thoughts.

"Are you telling me that Roxanne and Peter are actually under cover spies?" I watched both men as they merely nodded. "And that Lisa, as a child of these spies, was sent to the Franklin School to be programmed as a second generation spy?" The incredulousness oozed from my voice.

Finally, my godfather spoke up. "I'm sorry, Stephan, but that is *exactly* what we're telling you."

•　　•　　•

I was reeling, both literally and figuratively. I felt as if I'd been punched in the gut and couldn't catch my breath. The room, together with my world, was spinning. It was a good thing I was sitting down.

"That's just not possible," were the only words that would escape my throat.

In response, Director Ferguson slid a file across his desk in my direction. Apparently, he had been expecting my reaction, or something similar, since the file was somehow sitting on his desk, instead of having to have been pulled from a drawer.

I shakily reached for the folder, opened it, and saw a photocopy of what appeared to be a report written in Russian. Behind it was a translation in English. Not bothering with the translation, I went back to the Russian version and read it. Then, I read it again. To satisfy some morbid curiosity, I reviewed the translation, just to assure myself that it was accurate. It was.

The document at which I was looking was a report from a Captain Yuri Ovechkin to a Colonel Leonid Pushkin. Highlighted, for what I had to assume was my benefit, was the portion of the report detailing the programming progress of a very young Lisa Jones. It stated that, "Young Ms. Jones shows tremendous potential, both from an intelligence standpoint and a receptivity standpoint. However, she also shows a higher ability to resist the programming after having been exposed numerous times. We have been assured that this latter issue will be dealt with."

My fingers ceased operating, and the file fell to the floor, where it lay open and mocking. I stared at my bosses, unseeing. When at last I could speak, all I was able to eek out was, "How?"

Director Ferguson took up the narrative. "Lisa's parents were willing participants, but we think that Lisa, and the other children of the spies, were, and are, unaware of what had been done to them."

I remained silent, intent on listening and learning as much as possible.

"We started looking at the school early on, before we knew of its connection to the deep cover program. The reason we looked at it was because we became aware that Captain Ovechkin was an occasional visitor, and if he had a hand in something, that meant Pushkin couldn't be too far behind, and where Pushkin went, trouble and death followed. We were never able to come up with anything that led us to pursue it further. Once the end of the Soviet Union came about, and détente followed, our focus was directed elsewhere."

I looked at my godfather for any telltale signs of anything amiss, but he was too much of a professional to give anything away.

"If that was the case, how did you find out what was happening at the school?" I was glad to hear a coherent question come out of me, as it reassured me that my mind was finally beginning to come back to life in a meaningful way.

"Let's just say that, not long ago, we came into possession of some documents, including the one you just read, that shed light on the entire enterprise."

"But if they scrapped the deep cover project, as you said earlier, what's with the Franklin School theme song and the hidden code? Why now?"

"Pushkin and Ovechkin are back. Pushkin as some kind of special liaison/business man and Ovechkin, if you can believe it, is the Russian Ambassador to the U.S. They've been very active in the States, which got me to thinking. What else could they be up to? One thing led to another, and here we are."

"And, by some coincidence, the recording made its way to me?" I tried not to let my skepticism show, but, being new to this spy thing, was not as adept as my godfather. What I did suddenly remember was my godfather's hug and admonition to *be careful*. I thought this might be a good time to heed that advice.

Instead of answering, Director Ferguson merely shrugged in silence.

In response to my own questions, I said, "No. I don't think it was coincidence after all." At that instant, I had an epiphany. I snapped my fingers and said, "Lisa! That's why you sent it to me."

I saw the Director glance at my godfather and make an internal decision. I looked at Dan and saw that he, too, saw what I saw, and was unaware of what that decision was.

"There's something else, too." He paused, as if weighing what, or how much, to tell me. I saw him look to my godfather, who, apparently, had figured out what the Director's next move was. Resignedly, he nodded in acquiescence. "This is going to come as a shock, but I think, because of what is going to be happening very soon, and the presence of both Pushkin and Ovechkin in D.C., it's important that you know." He again paused, although at this point I suspected it was more for dramatic effect than anything else. "Your parents were also part of the first wave of deep cover spies and came over with Lisa's parents."

I was back to reeling. I knew that what I had just heard was absolutely and irrefutably crazy, yet it hit me like a Mike Tyson right cross. In an effort to get my mind back under control, I took some deep breaths. I had felt as if I were getting a sense of understanding and didn't want that to slip away. I looked at my godfather, who stared back with what I could only describe as dead eyes.

Addressing Dan Fowler, I said, "You know that can't be true, Dan. My father was a lifer in the U.S. Air Force. He was your friend."

"I'm sorry, Stephan, but the man you call your father, while he may have been my friend, was not your biological father."

I couldn't sit still any longer. I bound from my chair and paced, running my fingers through my hair like a mad scientist from a 1950s science fiction B-Movie. They let me, as what I just heard began to take hold. As I returned to my chair and sat once again, I poured another glass of water and gulped it down, struggling to get my mind under control.

"Tell me," was all I said to Dan.

Before responding, he looked to his boss for confirmation, which was received in the form of a silent nod.

"Your parents had become disillusioned with their mission and had approached the US government. They wanted to disappear with you, their only child, and live in peace. They felt that their government had lied to them, and in their dealings with us, they became, shall we say, less than trustful with their overseers. The U.S. gave them money, which they used to run. Unfortunately, the Russians got wind of their betrayal and Pushkin sent a team. They ran during a violent rainstorm and were driven off the road and left for dead. We had our own man following. When he came upon the wreck, he found your parents dead and you injured in the back seat. The crash had broken your leg. He rescued you just before your parent's car exploded. He and his wife had always wanted a child but were unable to conceive. The government made it look like a standard adoption and instead of Steven, they changed your name to Stephan, just to make you their own and not to be too confusing for you."

Unconsciously, I reached down and rubbed my leg, finally understanding the source of both the pain and the nightmares. At that moment, knowing didn't help much. I gaped at Dan Fowler, shaking my head. "You knew this the whole time. Knew that my entire life was a lie."

"It was for the best, Stephan."

"Bastard," was all I could think to say.

Finally, Director Ferguson took control. "Stephan, I know all of this is a lot to process. And I know you're probably pissed as hell."

I interrupted, not caring. "That's an understatement."

The Director ignored the intrusion and continued. "But," he said, not missing a beat, "there are more important issues at hand."

He waited until I refocused on him. "And those are?" My tone didn't border on insubordination, it ran over those borders and obliterated them. Under the circumstances, he overlooked that.

"We are offering you a chance to save Lisa."

That statement worked like a slap across the face to a fainted damsel in distress in that same B-Movie. I sat up straighter and said, "Is she in some kind of danger?"

"We think so. Our information is that something is going down tonight at an event to be held at the Russian embassy. We think Lisa has been programmed to make some kind of attempt on the life of the Vice-President."

"Wait. My Lisa? An assassination attempt? She's definitely not a shooter. There must be some mistake."

"It's not that kind of attempt. It's more of a scientific assassination, and she's definitely a scientist," my *godfather* chimed in, causing my head to snap around in his direction.

"What does that even mean?" I asked.

The Director once again took over. "The science behind it is unimportant, and, frankly, beyond our understanding," indicating those of us in the room. "What is important is that we have secured an invitation for you to attend this event and stop it."

"Send in the troops!" I shouted. "Why leave it to one person without the proper training?"

"Think about it, Stephan."

Suddenly, it dawned on me. We couldn't send in the troops without starting a war. The realization was apparent on my face and not lost on the others.

"Exactly," said the Director. "Plus, you have a personal stake in the matter, it being Lisa who is being used. Also, there is the matter of Pushkin."

"What about him?" I asked.

"He's going to be at the event. So will Ambassador Ovechkin."

"So, I'll be face-to-face with the people responsible for murdering my parents?"

"You will be," was the reply, as he held out an envelope.

I accepted the envelope and noticed the fancy calligraphy. Inside was a formal invitation to attend a pre-opening of an exhibition of historic Russian art and artifacts. The date was today, in about ninety minutes.

"We'll have a driver take you to the hotel so you can get cleaned up. He'll wait and take you to the event."

The Director stood and held out his hand, clearly demonstrating that this meeting was over. Dan and I followed suit. I reached for the Director's hand and found my eyes drifting to that Roland Voice Transformer. The Director seemed not to have noticed.

I pocketed the invitation and turned to face Dan Fowler. He held his hand out, but I couldn't bring myself to accept it. I felt totally betrayed. I walked away from him without saying a word, remembering what he'd said when we'd last parted company. "*Be careful.*"

●　　　●　　　●

As soon as Stephan had left the office, Fowler turned to Director Ferguson and said, "Want to tell me what you're thinking? I don't recall telling him his origin story being part of the plan."

Director Ferguson turned and reached into the cubby of his credenza, removed the Roland Voice Transformer and placed it on the desk.

"What's that?"

"That is a state-of-the-art voice transformer. When I came into the office, I'm pretty sure Stephan was going over to check it out. Later, I noticed him eyeing it again, which is unfortunate."

"Why?" asked Fowler, not understanding the significance.

"Because I'm not sure how convinced he was and because he's not completely stupid."

Fowler finally understood. "He had that recording and it was a disguised voice."

"Exactly. And, at some point, he's going to put two and two together. I needed him as off-balance as possible. I don't want him thinking clearly about any of this. It's better if he focuses on saving his girlfriend and the possibility of exacting some sort of revenge on the Russians."

"Shit," was Fowler's understated response. "That is unfortunate."

LISA AND THE EVENT

Lisa was at home, sitting at her kitchen table and holding a very fancy envelope with beautiful calligraphy. She opened the envelope and removed an equally impressive invitation to the pre-opening of a very prestigious event: the long awaited exhibition of a treasure trove of old Russian art and artifacts. She'd heard about the event from people both able to get tickets and wishing they could, but nobody she knew had been invited to the pre-opening. It was quite the coup, although she couldn't recall the circumstances which led to the invitation in hand. It bothered her, a little, but, she thought, "*Let's not look a gift horse in the mouth.*" Even after having removed the invitation from the envelope, it had more heft than it should for an empty envelope. She turned the envelope upside-down and was rewarded by the thunk of something hitting the table: a computer data stick.

She inspected it for any markings or labeling, and finding none, murmured to herself, "What the hell is this?" Having no idea, she placed the stick on top of the envelope and checked the time. Realizing that time was short, she'd set about to begin the laborious process of getting ready.

In her bedroom, she saw a bag hanging on her closet door and remembered the sleek black dress she had purchased for the occasion, together with a small handbag and black shoes with a touch of sparkle. The sight reminded her of the shopping trip and brought a slight smile to her lips, although it was accompanied by an uneasy feeling. She shrugged and began to undress for the shower when her phone buzzed. She found it, saw that the number of the caller was blocked and was about to throw it on her bed, unanswered, when some inner voice told her to answer. Unable to resist that inner voice, she connected the call and brought the speaker to her ear. Beeps, buzzes, hisses, and musical notes greeted her as soon as she answered, no longer masked by the school theme song. At the first sound, she relaxed so much that she couldn't help but sit on the edge of her bed, which was, luckily, within easy reach. It was a brief message and, when it was over, she disconnected the call, rose, and gently placed the phone on her bedside nightstand. She retrieved the data stick and made her way to her computer, where she inserted the stick into the waiting port. Greeted by beeps, buzzes, hisses, and musical notes, she raptly listened to her final instructions. The message ended, and she removed the stick from its port, replacing it on the table. She took a deep breath and, revived, returned to her bedroom and walked crisply to the new dress. She inspected it and, visibly pleased, smiled as she went into the bathroom to shower so she would not be late for the exhibition.

"I'm so looking forward to this!" she exclaimed before letting the hot water wash over her body.

•　　•　　•

Unlike many embassies on what has come to be known as "Embassy Row," which are mostly housed in old mansions, the Russian Embassy was located at 2650 Wisconsin Ave NW, in what was known as Boris Nemtsov Plaza, within view of the Capitol, the White House, the Pentagon and the State Department. It was a complex of buildings, the main building being ten-stories in height and looking much like an office building. The entire compound sat behind an ornate wrought-iron fence which sat atop a stone wall. Instead of a sidewalk, in front of the electronic gates, was a large paved plaza which was used, on occasions such as this evening, as a drop-off point for the many cabs, private cars, and limousines. Security being a major concern, they permitted no cars onto the grounds and no guests were permitted to enter without first having their invitations scanned, their bags checked, and their persons "wanded."

Lisa exited her cab and stood among the throngs of others lucky enough to have been invited. She felt somewhat like an impostor, not being a member of the Washington elite, but thought to herself, *"Fuck it, I'm going to enjoy this."* She was swept along with the crowd and willingly submitted to the security procedures, having nothing to hide. Since the distance from the gate to the entrance of the main building was considerable, the consulate had golf carts available for transporting those not well enough or too lazy to make the trek under their own power. Lisa chose to walk, taking in the fresh air and people watching, to her great delight. When she was a hundred feet or so from the entrance, her phone rang. She reached into her handbag, pulled it out, and, without hesitation, answered the call. The phone to her ear, she stopped in her tracks as the unmasked beeps, buzzes, hisses, and musical notes filled her consciousness. She listened for a few moments, to the great annoyance of those walking behind her, before disconnecting the call and replacing the phone in her bag. When she continued on her way to the entrance, it was with a renewed vigor and completely oblivious to the looks from those having to detour around her.

After waiting in line to enter the building, Lisa, along with everyone else, was forced to submit to another round of security checks. A wand, metal detector and x-ray machine, to say nothing of the facial recognition cameras scanning each guest. She approached the metal detector, placed her handbag in the plastic container waiting on the x-ray machine's conveyor belt, and smiled at the camera. Passing through the metal detector without an alarm sounding, she awaited her handbag, which had stopped in the machine as it was being inspected. The Russian woman attending the machine motioned to a female comrade, who came over, took the handbag, and opened it. Removing a perfume bottle, she approached Lisa and, in heavily accented English, asked, "Is this yours?"

Lisa, having seen it being removed from her bag, replied, "Yes, it is."

"Please, what is in it?"

Amused, Lisa said, "It's perfume."

The guard held the bottle out for Lisa and said, "Please, to put it on you."

Lisa accepted the bottle and, without hesitation, sprayed a little on each wrist, taking a moment to bring each wrist to her nose and sniff the aroma.

Smiling, Lisa held the bottle out to her interrogator and asked, "Would you like to try some?"

Not amused, the guard scowled, reached for Lisa's handbag, and motioned for her to enter. Accepting the handbag, she returned the bottle and jauntily moved forward to the exhibition.

STEPHAN GOES TO THE EXHIBITION

Due to the last minute nature of my "assignment," Homeland had sprung for a hotel room so that I would have some place to change clothes and sleep. It wasn't the Ritz, but it was definitely nicer than I would have gotten had I been paying for it. My driver, a young probationary agent named Tim, had dropped me off and told me he would be waiting out front whenever I was ready.

I was glad for the solitude of my hotel room. After everything I'd just heard, I needed to regain my composure and think clearly. It was obvious to me that I was being used in some fashion. I just couldn't yet figure out in what way. If what I had been told was true, and I had to assume that at least some of the information was correct, Lisa had a part to play in whatever awaited at the embassy. If I could "save" her, whatever that meant under the circumstances, I needed to be at the top of my game. While I was certain that the Director and that *bastard* godfather felt something would go down at the exhibition, I was uncertain that they knew exactly what or, even if they did, that it would occur as they had envisioned. So, I knew I needed to be ready for almost anything.

Learning that my entire life had been a lie, and that my godfather, a man who was supposed to be looking out for my well-being, had known and abetted this lie, caused me to rethink everything I knew about him. I'd always thought I could trust him, but the knowledge of his willingness and ability to lie to me, as well as the jobs he'd had, including at Homeland, made me reassess that thought. He was a highly trained and efficient liar who had taken an oath to protect his country above all else. For all I knew, his "friendship" with my father could have been a cover so he could keep tabs on me. True, he hadn't had me arrested, but was that just because I might serve a useful purpose? I had to believe that I couldn't believe anything or trust anybody. Maybe the best piece of advice he ever gave to me was when I'd left his house that last time: *be careful.* I'm not sure he meant it to apply to himself, but that is definitely the way I was taking it. In my mind I added the unspoken words, "*trust no one, especially me.*"

So, if I couldn't trust them to have told me the entire truth, what could I believe and what could I do with it? That they had entrusted this to me, an untrained pseudo-operative on the job for a few hours, had all sorts of alarm bells going off in my psyche. What it told me was that I was intended to fail. Which, in turn, told me that Lisa was intended to succeed. But could she, in fact, be an assassin, even an unwilling one? My entire being told me it just wasn't possible, but I also knew that there was a wealth of scientific knowledge of which I was unaware. So, if she had in fact been "programmed," and if she in fact did not know and was unaware of her mission, I suppose it would be possible. Damn!

Mission. The word jarred a memory. When I was attempting to decipher the intercepted message, the first word I was able to translate was, "*mission.*" Later, when I finally broke through, I translated, "*you have a limited time to complete.*" Putting them together, I surmised the message was, "*you have a limited time to complete your mission.*" But what was it about the statement? I racked my brain until, finally, I realized that the phrase "*you have a limited time to complete*" had not been spoken in a human voice It was a *mechanically altered* voice! It didn't seem relevant at the time and I didn't focus on it, but at this moment it struck me like a slap across the face!

My internal dialogue was going at warp speed. Why would a Director at the Office of Homeland Security have a Roland Voice Transformer model VT4? Don't they have a separate department or division to handle sending clandestine messages? And, if they were going to do it, would they bother using a commercially available machine, no matter how good it was? I was certain that Homeland had capabilities beyond anything I could imagine when it came to disguising not only voices, but identities. Plus, the message was in *Russian*, not English. No, it was something else. Why would someone need to use a voice transformer? Because they don't want their voice recognized. Duh. Why would somebody fear someone might recognize their voice? Because they knew what programs were listening and what might trigger closer scrutiny!

I slammed my fist into the nearest inanimate object. Thankfully, it was a pillow, and I didn't do any damage to myself.

Director Ferguson was behind the message! Which could only mean that Dan Fowler, that bastard, knew what was going on and agreed to get me involved, anyway. Which also meant that both Lisa and I were pawns and in greater danger than we could imagine.

I jumped from my seat, grabbed my jacket and the invitation, stuffed my phone into a pocket, and sprinted from my room to the elevator. I didn't know what was really going on or how to stop it, but I knew for certain that Lisa and I were part of the endgame and time was definitely of the essence.

•   •   •

I exited the building and searched frantically for Tim and the car. He must have seen me from wherever he waited, because moments later, he pulled to a stop right in front of me. I yanked the door open, jumped into the back seat behind him, and screamed, "Go, go, go! We need to hurry!"

Tim remained calm and looked at me through the rear-view mirror, trying to assess my mental condition, which, I'm sure, was easy to ascertain. I was frantic, panicked, and appeared more than a little crazy.

"Sir, are you OK?"

I returned his gaze through the mirror while trying to calm myself, or at least present the appearance of calmness. "Yes, Tim. I'm fine. We just really need to hurry." Seeing that he wasn't totally convinced, I added, as calmly as I could, "Please."

He nodded to himself and gently pulled away from the building and entered the flow of traffic. As trained, he was being careful to observe traffic laws. I wanted to scream at him again, "For God's sake, man, move!" I restrained myself, not wanting him to make an unscheduled detour to the local psych ward.

Outwardly, I remained calm looking, or so I thought. Internally, I was a mess. My mind couldn't escape the loop which it had entered, namely that Ferguson and Fowler were responsible for whatever was about to happen. I prayed I wouldn't be too late.

I laid my head back against the seat, closed my eyes and took deep breaths in an effort to get myself under control. I thought it was working.

WHAM!

The entire car shuddered and was pushed sideways, the tires offering no resistance. In my haste to get into the car and get moving, I had neglected to fasten my seatbelt. As a result, and because I was trying to relax and unaware of any impending danger, my body went with the flow, in accordance with the laws of physics. It threw me from the left side of the car, clear against the passenger door on the right side. Somehow, the car continued to slide, as if still being pushed, which didn't seem to make sense. I turned my head to the left and saw the front end of a garbage truck still embedded in that side of the car and actively engaged in shoving the car as far as possible. As soon as we hit the embankment, the car tilted on its side, balanced for a moment, and succumbed to gravity, tumbling down the side of a small ravine as I held onto the door handle with one hand and the front seat headrest with the other. When we came to an abrupt halt, I could barely move. I felt something drip into my eye and wiped it away, my hand coming away bloodied. I must have hit my head on something, but had no memory of it. It seemed to me that the car was still in motion, although that may have been the final rocking motion as it came to rest. I looked for Tim and found him slumped over sideways, held in place by his seatbelt. He was covered in the white powder that erupted from the steering wheel airbag, blood coloring the whiteness like some sick Jackson Pollock painting. I called his name, the sound of my voice sounding painfully amplified in the close confines of the wreck. He didn't answer, but I could see his chest slowly rising and falling as he continued to breathe. Testing myself for broken parts, I was pleasantly surprised that I could move without excruciating pain. I turned my head and was able to see out one window, which was pointed upward towards the street. Someone, a man, was standing and gazing at the wreckage, giving me hope he would summon help. Instead, he nodded to himself and slowly walked away without another glance at us.

I gathered my wits as best I could and remembered where I was going and what I needed to accomplish. Seeing the man walk away made me realize one thing: this was no accident, and Ferguson and Fowler had somehow concluded that I had figured out the relevant parts of their scheme. If I was suddenly expendable, that meant Lisa was in more danger than ever.

I maneuvered my body so that I could push my back against the front seat and kick at the rear window with both legs. After approximately a million kicks, the window burst from its frame and I scrambled my way through and out into the night air. I patted myself down and found that my phone and the invitation hadn't moved. Smoothing my clothes down with one hand and my hair with the other, I hobbled away just as the sounds of approaching sirens became audible.

BACK AT THE EXHIBITION

The exhibition was being held in the large ballroom known as the "Golden Hall." Centrally located within the confines of the large main building, its walls were covered with labor intensive and, as a result, expensive, enamel paintings, a rather ostentatious display for a country that once prided itself in being for the "working man." The ceiling was adorned with romanticized depictions of traditional Russian subjects: fields of grasses, cereals, fruits, and berries, and the workers required to plant and harvest each. A very Russian space for a very Russian exhibit.

They had lined the room with display cases, together with various displays, throughout the vast expanse of the open, yet columnated, space. On display were Faberge eggs, jewels of the Czars, paintings by Wassily Kandinsky, Kazimir Malevich, Aleksander Rodchenko, and other Russian masters, plus countless other items hoarded by the government.

Servers strolled through the well-dressed crowd offering various Russian hors d'oeuvres, including caviar, as well as glasses of champagne. Lisa meandered through the exhibits with the crowd, looking as if she belonged. Ambassador Ovechkin, dressed in a tuxedo for the occasion, circulated through the room, mingling with the various dignitaries with whom he was acquainted and meeting new ones as if he'd known them his entire life, playing the consummate host. Mr. Pushkin, having no official presence other than as the liaison with the Smithsonian, chatted amiably with Cheryl Rosen, who had been able to observe some objects prior to being displayed, Pushkin having been able to accommodate her request, as least to the point where it appeared to be cooperation.

As Lisa made her way through the room, a server approached carrying a tray of canapes. She stopped in front of Lisa and asked, "Would you like a napkin, Miss?"

Lisa, not surprised by the intrusion, held out her hand and said, "Yes, thank you."

Ignoring the small paper napkins which lay within easy reach on the edge of her tray, the server reached into her apron pocket with her free hand and removed a white dinner napkin, rolled as if to have been placed at a dining table place setting. She placed it in Lisa's waiting palm, turned and walked away to continue her rounds.

As soon as the napkin touched her palm, Lisa closed her hand around it, feeling the solidity and weight of the solid object hidden within. The object secure in her hand, she continued on her way, unnoticed.

The Vice President of the United States, together with two secret service body guards, attempting, and failing to look nonchalant, approached Ambassador Ovechkin and was greeted warmly.

"Mr. Vice President, I'm so glad you could make it." Shaking hands with his honored guest, Ovechkin looked around, as if searching for someone, and said, "I don't see Mrs. Hobbs. Was she not able to join us this evening?" The disappointment was meant to be conveyed and seemed heartfelt.

"Mr. Ambassador, no, I'm afraid she was not feeling well and thought it best to come another time, that is, if you can accommodate her."

"Of course, we'd be very happy to arrange a visit. Please, just give me a call and I will personally make the arrangements."

"That's very kind of you. Thank you."

"Of course. It will be my pleasure. Now, please enjoy the exhibition. I have matters to attend to." He gave a slight bow and took his leave of the Vice President, moving to have a conversation with the Japanese Ambassador, who had just arrived.

Ever the consummate politician, the Ambassador continued to make his rounds until an aide approached and discreetly whispered in his ear, after which he made his way to the microphone which stood in front of the four-piece chamber ensemble, who had ceased their playing as the Ambassador approached.

Tapping the microphone, the room was filled with the resultant loud thumping noise, causing the desired cessation of conversation.

Looking sheepish, the Ambassador said, "I guess this thing is on."

He was greeted with the expected polite laughter.

"Esteemed guests, it is my great pleasure to welcome you tonight. My country has a long and illustrious history in the arts. Most of what you will have the pleasure of viewing this evening has not been available to the public for seventy years or more. We hope you enjoy our treasures and that this exhibition serves as a continuation of a mutual sharing of the arts. Thank you and enjoy the evening."

The response was a generous round of applause, which seemed to delight the Ambassador, who seemed totally in his element. As he continued to mingle, he saw Pushkin and made his way to him. Pushkin excused himself from his current conversation and joined his old compatriot.

Surveying the room, Pushkin said, "Quite the turnout."

"Yes, not bad at all." Joining his friend in his survey, he added, "there may even be a few that aren't spies."

Chuckling, Pushkin said, "Maybe a few."

As they continued to scan the room in silence, Pushkin's gaze rested on the far side of the room, as he said, "Speaking of spies, look over there," motioning with his head.

Following his old bosses' eyes, he spotted Bob Ferguson and Dan Fowler as they each reached for a glass of champagne from a passing server.

With a mischievous twinkle in his eye, Ovechkin said, "It's always such a pleasure to see them. Let's go over and say hello."

Pushkin smiled and replied, "Yes, let's," motioning for the Ambassador to lead the way. Together, they maneuvered through the sea of bodies until they stood face to face with their former enemies.

Taking the lead, Ambassador Ovechkin tilted his head in acknowledgment and said, "Gentlemen, I wasn't aware that either of you were lovers of the arts, especially Russian art."

In unison, they each raised their glass in mock salute, as Director Ferguson said, "We couldn't pass up an opportunity like this."

"It doesn't look like we were alone in taking advantage of this opportunity," said Fowler, taking in the room with his eyes.

"No, it's quite the turnout," said Pushkin. "We're very pleased to see such a high interest in our heritage."

Before either of the Americans could respond, two stern looking men, obviously part of the Russian security detail, approached the two Russians. One leaned over and spoke in low tones to the Ambassador, as the other remained vigilantly reviewing his surroundings.

The conversation completed, Ovechkin turned to Ferguson and Fowler and said, "Gentlemen, you'll have to excuse us. Enjoy the evening."

The Americans both nodded at their hosts and again raised their glasses to their retreating backs. They glanced at each other, as if to silently say, "*I wonder what that was about*," before they turned and began their own circulation of the room.

As Pushkin and Ovechkin followed the security men, a loud clatter was heard on the far side of the room as a server dropped his tray of champagne glasses, shouted something unintelligible, and rushed towards the Vice President of the United States.

· · ·

After I'd limped away from the wreckage, I made my way to a social path which led back up the embankment. It was slow going for me, but was far enough away from the wreckage so that, in the twilight of evening, I passed unnoticed. I moved to a paved sidewalk and stopped to get my bearings. As I walked, I glimpsed myself in a passing store window. I was not a pretty sight. I ducked inside a crowded restaurant, making my way through the waiting bodies to the men's room in the back. Once inside, I was able to use the facilities, clean the blood from my face, and water my hair down so that it didn't look as if I'd been caught in a Tesla coil. Thankfully, the blood on the wound had coagulated enough that it shouldn't pose a dripping problem. I'd straightened myself up enough so that I didn't feel self-conscience being in public. Once I'd exited the restaurant, I had to get my bearings and figure out where the Russian embassy was. I used the GPS on my phone and determined that I was close enough to walk, which would probably be faster in the long-run than trying to flag down a cab and fight traffic. I noted the route and determinedly headed off in the direction of the embassy, trying to hurry and not limp too much.

It took about twenty minutes, but I finally arrived at my destination. I made my way through the various security stations with no problems. Not knowing if wearing civilian clothing would make a difference, I decided not to chance it and had decided not to be in uniform for whatever awaited. I entered the already crowded room, obviously one of the last to arrive. Moving around as stealthily as possible, I walked and scanned, my head unconsciously turning to and fro with the rhythm of the music. I was frantic to spot Lisa, but not knowing what she was wearing made it difficult in the sea of formal black gowns. I thought I saw Fowler and Ferguson moving away from me, but couldn't be certain. As much as I wanted to confront them, my focus had to remain on finding Lisa.

Suddenly, I heard a commotion coming from the other side of the room. It sounded as if somebody had dropped a serving tray, and, based on the breaking of glass, it had been filled with glasses of champagne. Instead of the applause such an event would have earned in a high school cafeteria, what followed was a loud, guttural cry. All eyes turned in the direction of the scream, mine being powerless not to join. What I saw did not quite compute. It looked like a maniacal version of Leonard rushing towards a man who, in response, was being pushed down by two men flanking him. Frantically, I searched for Lisa, thinking this was either the attempt that Ferguson had talked about, or a diversion. The resultant panic didn't make my searching any easier, as I was swept up in the multitude of bodies moving away from the man being protected. At the last moment, before turning in the crowd's direction, I saw Lisa calmly trying to walk against the crowd toward the man being surrounded, who must have been the Vice President. I called to her, but she either hadn't heard me or, in her "programmed" state, ignored me and continued her slow progress toward the Vice President.

•　•　•

At the sound of the commotion, Ferguson and Fowler, like everybody else, turned to see what was happening. Instead of making a move in any particular direction, they shared a quick smile and perused their surroundings. A shocked look overtook Ferguson's face as he spotted Stephan Beck in the crowd, visibly seeking Lisa's whereabouts. He pointed Stephan out to Fowler, who quietly said, "What the...?" in bewilderment.

Recovering from his astonishment, Ferguson looked for the men he'd posted throughout the room, made eye contact with one, and signaled in the direction of Stephan, nodding his head in the affirmative. The agent made his way to one of the many fluted columns in the room, never losing sight of his prey. When in position, he surreptitiously removed a silenced pistol from a shoulder holster and waited for a clear shot.

•   •   •

As soon as Leonard had dropped his tray and run towards the Vice President, the Secret Service detail sprang into action. One man removed a gun from his holster and faced the threat as the other used his left arm to push his charge to the floor, while, with his right hand, he reached into his coat pocket and removed a small spray bottle, which he quickly used to spray into the air directly in front of the Vice President's nose before replacing it and substituting his weapon and searching for threats.

•   •   •

Many years of operational experience had taught Pushkin that, while in the field, not everything was as it appeared. Instead of focusing his attention in the direction of the scream, he turned to scan the rest of the room, just in time to notice the slight smile on the lips of Director Ferguson. His attention thusly focused, he also followed Ferguson's gaze when he'd spotted Stephan, saw the look of astonishment on Ferguson's face, and the silent directions to his agent. Immediately, he responded in kind, using the hidden communication device running down the inside of his jacket sleeve to dispatch a Russian security man toward Ferguson's would be assassin.

As Pushkin watched the scene unfold, he drew his attention back to the man who had so surprised Ferguson, seeing him intently focused on a woman who, against all odds, was pushing against the crowd and moving in the direction of the Vice President. Puzzled by the situation, he thought to himself, *"What the hell is in play?"* In that moment, he turned to see Ferguson's agent lining up a shot with a silenced weapon, clearly aiming for the surprise guest. Seeing that his man would not reach the assassin in time, he calmly spoke into his microphone. Moments later, the weaponized agent silently slid down the column, coming to his ultimate resting place, a throwing knife lodged deeply into his neck.

•   •   •

I was too far away to reach Lisa, especially as I was being pushed in the opposite direction. I saw a secret service agent, gun in hand, searching the room for a target, and knew he'd spot Lisa at any moment. If a lone person fighting the crowd on her way to the Vice President during utter chaos wasn't suspicious, nothing was. To make matters worse, I noticed something white in her hand, light reflecting off something metallic peeking out of the end. I was certain the Secret Service agent would have noticed it, too.

I racked my brain for a solution to what seemed like an unsolvable problem. Come on!

The conversation I'd had with Ferguson and Fowler flashed through my mind. Lisa, Leonard and countless others had been programmed. They responded to Russian, even though they didn't understand it. I spoke Russian. I needed Lisa to hear me, but I needed the trigger before she would pay attention. The trigger! That was it!

I pushed against the crowd toward where the chamber ensemble had been playing. All had fled the stage, taking their precious instruments but leaving the microphone. Crazed with fright, I was terrified I wouldn't make it in time and they would gun Lisa down, branded an attempted assassin. I pushed and shoved my way towards the microphone, knocking some people, both men and women, onto the floor so that I could step over them on my way to what I hoped would be my electronic salvation. When I finally reached my destination, I searched for my phone, never taking my eyes from Lisa, who continued her slow but steady progress towards death. The phone suddenly in hand, I had no choice but to lose sight of her as I searched through files, looking for the recording made at the Franklin School reunion and which was the cause of so much trouble and death. Hands shaking, I finally found what I was looking for, opened the file and, bringing the phone to the microphone, which I could only hope remained turned on, hit "play." Instantly, the sounds of *La Voltaire et La Franklein* filled the room. I couldn't hear the sounds hidden in the background, but I knew they were there. My eyes found Lisa, who, at the sound of the music, came to a standstill, giving me the hope and time I needed. I shouted into the microphone, "PRERVAT'! PRERVAT'! PRERVAT'! (Abort! Abort! Abort!)."

I held my breath as all sound seemed to leave the room and everything moved in slow motion. Lisa was looking around in a daze, as if she had no idea where she was or how she'd gotten there. She looked at her hand, saw it held something, and released it, watching as a small khanjali, a specialized Russian dagger, slipped from the napkin and fell to the floor. I saw similar reactions from one of the secret service agents, Leonard, and a few other people scattered throughout the room.

Once time returned to normal, I rushed to Lisa and held her in my arms, the bewildered look on her face enough to break my heart.

•   •   •

In the commotion, Ferguson and Fowler attempted to follow the crowd and make their way to the exit. Having been alerted by Pushkin, the security team stopped them before they could escape into the night. They were promptly marched to where Pushkin waited, Ovechkin having gone to check on the Vice President. Pushkin said nothing, waiting for the Ambassador to return from his visit to the Vice President, who was, to all appearances, doing well, if shaken up a little. After the Ambassador and Vice President had spoken, the Vice President glanced in the direction of

Ferguson and Fowler, curtly nodded, and was led by his Secret Service detail from the room to his waiting limousine.

Ferguson and Fowler were both seething as they waited for the Ambassador to return, although they said nothing. Upon his return, Ovechkin said to the Americans, "You two seemed to be in such a hurry, just when it was getting interesting." He looked at Pushkin before turning back to his former nemeses. "Something tells me you won't be leaving anytime soon."

Ferguson looked at him, bewildered. "What the fuck are you talking about?" He looked at Fowler and said, "Let's go," as he tried to turn and walk away. They were halted in their tracks by the iron grip of a waiting security team member. Trying to shake them off, Ferguson said, "What the fuck do you think you're doing? You can't keep us here. We're still American citizens in America."

Ovechkin and Pushkin looked at each other, letting Ferguson's word sink in. Suddenly, both started to laugh. Genuine laughs, not the fake laughs used to aggravate Ferguson and Fowler in the past. The Americans looked on in total bewilderment.

"What's so funny? All I need to do is make one phone call and we're out of here so fast you won't know we were ever here." Ferguson reached for his phone and tried to use his thumb to unlock it, before having it unceremoniously ripped from his grasp by a guard and handed to Ovechkin.

Pushkin looked at Ovechkin and said, "They really don't get it."

"No, it seems they don't." Turning his attention back to Ferguson and Fowler, he said, "Let me explain your situation." He pointed to the dead agent still leaning against the column. "You attempted to commit a capital crime in Russia."

"Now I know you're out of your mind. First, I don't know who that man is, or was. Second, in case you haven't noticed, we're not in Russia, you crazy bastard! We're in the good 'ole U. S. of A. So, I'm not going to tell you again, let us go!"

Ovechkin ignored the ranting and continued. "Please. Look at your surroundings. Does this look like the good 'ole U. S. of A. to you?" Ovechkin took a menacing step closer to Ferguson and said, "Fucking idiot! You are in the Russian embassy, which, for all intents and purposes, *is* Russia. The two of you may as well be in the Kremlin. The only rights you have are those we allow you to have."

As Ovechkin's words hit home, the former American spymasters staggered backwards under the weight of the truth, finally beginning to realize the seriousness of their predicament.

Fowler recovered enough to say, "You don't have proof of any crime, so you have no reason to hold us."

Pushkin held his hand out to the security agent sent to dispatch the would be American assassin. Immediately, he was handed the dead agent's credentials, which he opened, momentarily perused, and held out for Ferguson and Fowler to see. They glanced at it for a mere fraction of a second before disavowing any knowledge of the agent or his mission.

Ovechkin continued, ignoring the denials. "And then there is the matter of Ms. Jones and Mr. Beck." Everybody turned to see them in a still, silent embrace, both appearing to weep.

"No idea what you're talking about," said Ferguson.

Still ignoring any protestation from his prisoners, Ovechkin turned and pointed to a woman standing to the side of the room, quietly drinking a glass of champagne. At the sight, Ferguson's face fell.

"I believe you are acquainted with Ms. Cook."

Ferguson could not help but look in her direction. Catching his eye, she smiled and raised her glass in salute. All fight seeped out of Ferguson. Fowler, realizing who she was, became resigned to his fate. Summoning something from deep inside himself, Ferguson made one last attempt at improving his position. "You know our government will never let you just keep us."

Ovechkin, still amused, said, "Under most circumstances, I'd agree with you. But, this is not most circumstances. I've had a nice little chat with your Vice President and they are most eager for this whole matter to go away and not become a major incident. You are both, it would seem, ours to do with as we please."

Addressing his security men, the Ambassador took great pleasure in saying, "Take them downstairs and lock them up. We'll deal with them later." He turned to where Stephan and Lisa still stood. "It seems as if we have some unfinished business to deal with."

• • •

We stood embracing one another, crying tears of joy and relief, for an eternity. At some point, I looked over to see Ferguson and Fowler, who I still thought of as my godfather (old habits die hard), being detained by some Russian security people. The other people were unknown to me, but they looked as if they had some authority. I loosened my embrace enough to look Lisa in the eyes and said, "We need to go over there," motioning with my head. She didn't bother to ask why, just nodded and said, "OK."

We turned and, as we walked towards the group of men, saw the two Russians with apparent authority laugh, resulting in both Ferguson and Fowler being overcome with dejection. "*Good!*" I thought to myself. I saw the two Russians look in our direction just before the security men escorted the Americans away, firm grips on one arm of each.

As we approached, I pointed to the men being led away and quietly said to Lisa, "They're the ones behind this whole thing."

The surprise was evident in her reaction as she said, "The two Americans?"

"Yes."

We stood in front of the two Russians, saying nothing, until Lisa said, "I need some information from those two."

Pushkin responded by saying, "Very well." He turned in the direction in which Ferguson and Fowler were being led and said, in a loud authoritative voice, "Boris, just one minute. Bring them back here."

Boris and his fellow security team member promptly turned their prisoners around and marched them back to our position. Before Lisa could do or say anything, I stepped to Fowler and slapped him hard across his cheek. "You fucking bastard. I hope you and your friend here rot away in some jail, never to be heard from again."

My *former* godfather merely stood in silence as the outline of my fingers appeared on his face.

Lisa took a step forward and looked at me for guidance. I pointed to Ferguson. She addressed him. "I agree with Stephan's hopes, but first I need you to tell me where the antidote is."

Ferguson looked at Lisa and smiled. "Fuck you and your Russian spy mother."

Lisa looked at him uncomprehendingly.

I said to her, "It's a long story. I'll fill you in."

She took a step forward and, with all the fury she could muster, slapped Ferguson over and over until Pushkin gently pulled her away.

"Ms. Jones, I understand why you'd want to beat him, but please, just give me a moment."

He calmly moved forward and whispered into Ferguson's ear so quietly that none of us could make out what he said. When finished, he stepped away from Ferguson, who looked ghostly, the blood having drained from his face.

Pushkin nodded to him and Ferguson said, "Go see your good friend Jennifer."

Pushkin nodded to his security men, who roughly grabbed their detainees and led them away.

I watched them disappear from view, my emotions mixed, but led by gratitude at having them out of our lives.

The two men introduced themselves and it surprised me to see that the Ambassador was content to let Pushkin take control of the conversation.

Pushkin looked at Lisa and said, with genuine affection, "So like your mother. After all was said and done, she turned out to be one of my favorites."

"You know my mother?"

"Once upon a time, I did." Looking at me, he continued, "I'm sure that Mr. Beck will fill you in on the details." Keeping his gaze on me, he said, "And you, Mr. Beck. You look so like your father."

The rage in me growing over an injustice done to a man of which I had no memory, I balled my hands into fists, keeping them at my side, and took a step forward. Through gritted teeth, I said, "You mean the father you murdered and whom I never got to know?"

Pushkin stood his ground and maintained a calm demeanor, even in the face of what had to appear as murderous rage. He looked at my face and trembling fists and calmly said, "Mr. Beck, please do not try to do anything that you won't live to regret," drawing attention with his eyes to the remaining security men still in attendance, all poised to draw weapons at a moment's notice. He waited as I unfurled my fists, took a deep breath, and stepped out of his personal space. "Thank you. A wise decision." I could see his shoulders relax, unaware that they had shown tension. "Those were very different times. A man in my position had to make very difficult decisions, and that was one of them. Looking back, I'm sorry that you never had a chance to get to know your actual parents, but, at the time, it was necessary."

His graciousness took me completely by surprise and served to totally disarm me. I had no words in response, so merely nodded in recognition of his statement.

Pushkin looked to the Ambassador, who took over control of the conversation. "I'm sure you both have many questions. Unfortunately, the answers that you don't already have will need to remain buried." He looked at Lisa and said, "I'm certain that Mr. Beck has most of the information you might seek."

Lisa, still slightly dazed and definitely confused, nodded and said, "Thank you."

"Now, if you'll excuse us, as you might imagine, we have much to do."

I couldn't help but ask, "What's going to happen to them?"

"They will be our guests for quite some time, I'm sure. Don't concern yourself. Let's just say that the hopes you expressed earlier have a good chance of becoming a reality."

The Ambassador turned and left, accompanied by two of his security team, leaving us alone with Pushkin and two more security team members.

Pushkin stood and assessed us. He smiled and said, "Based on your performances tonight, I have every faith that you will both be fine. It shows me we chose well." He paused, considered what else to say, and decided that what had been said was sufficient. "We've put a car at your disposal. Yuri here will show you the way." He gave a slight bow and said, "Good night."

We were both overwhelmed and stood unmoving as he walked out of sight. Yuri quietly stepped forward and said, "If you'd follow me, I'll show you to your car."

We let ourselves be led into the night, hand in hand.

EPILOGUE

At 7:00 the next morning, after a long night of discussion and not much sleep, Lisa and I waited anxiously for the elevator doors to open. When they finally did, we stepped out into an ordinary-looking hallway of an ordinary apartment building and quickly stepped to the ordinary-looking door of apartment 4 C.

I knocked loudly on the door as Lisa stood to the side. I positioned myself directly in front of the peephole so the occupant could easily identify me. Hearing nothing from inside the apartment, I knocked again, even louder. I finally heard movement behind the closed door, together with loud muttering that sounded like *"What the fuck? Hold your horses."* As I stood silently waiting, I could see the peep hole darken, followed by the door chain being removed, the withdrawal of the deadbolt and the turning of the handle. The door opened and Jennifer, still groggy and in her pajamas, apparently having been woken by my knocking, stifled a yawn and said, "Stephan? What are you doing here so early?"

Instead of answering, I took a step back, and Lisa immediately took my place. Before Jennifer could react, Lisa took a step forward and, with all her weight behind her, landed a right cross on Jennifer's cheek, which knocked her off her feet and caused her to hit her head on the floor, knocking her out cold.

Impressed, I said, "Nice form."

She looked up at me, smiling, and replied, "Thank you for the lessons."

I stepped past Lisa, got behind Jennifer, and dragged her by her arms into the apartment while Lisa closed and locked the door. Before she regained consciousness, I set her in a kitchen chair, where Lisa used copious amounts of the duct tape I removed from my pocket to secure her in place. Using a scarf brought just for the occasion, Lisa gagged her, just to ensure that she didn't scream when she regained consciousness.

While we waited, I used the coffee maker, made a fresh pot, and poured cups for myself and Lisa.

"Do you think she hit her head too hard?" Lisa asked, ever the concerned friend.

I went to a cupboard, removed a glass and filled it with cold water. Stepping back to Jennifer, I said, "Let's find out," as I threw the water in Jennifer's face.

Immediately, she came awake, trying to sputter like a toy motorboat engine, but unable to do so as a result of the most efficient gag ever used in the history of gagging. Her reaction was so over-the-top that you'd think we'd water-boarded her, which, by the way, I had suggested. When she finally calmed down, she looked at both of us, the terror evident in her darting eyes. We said nothing for a full minute. When she attempted to make talking noises, Lisa stepped forward, held her hand up as if to slap her, and said, "Shut the fuck up, you traitorous bitch."

Hearing those words served two purposes: it shut her up and made her aware that we knew what she'd done.

Lisa stepped forward and got right in front of Jennifer's face. "I'm going to remove the gag and ask you some questions. If you scream, I'll knock your ass out again, but for a lot longer. Do you understand me?"

Jennifer, still terrified, vigorously nodded in the affirmative.

Lisa untied the gag, stood back, and said, "How could you? I thought we were friends."

When Jennifer opened her mouth to answer, Lisa held her hand up and said, "Don't bother trying to explain. That was a rhetorical question."

Instantly, Jennifer's mouth snapped shut.

"Now, here's a question I definitely want an answer to. Ready?" Again, Jennifer nodded. "Good, because I'm only going to ask this once, and I'll speak slowly, so there's no misunderstanding. Where. Is. The. Antidote?"

Not bothering to pretend she didn't know what Lisa was talking about, she volunteered, "In the freezer." When she began to say something else, Lisa just held up her hand, which was enough to stop any further talk.

Lisa walked to the freezer, opened it and, in the door, found two vials, each marked with Roxanne's name and the word "Antidote." She turned and displayed them to Jennifer, who volunteered, "That's it. That's all of it."

Lisa placed them in her purse, from which she removed a small plastic spray bottle. As she walked to Jennifer, Jennifer's eyes widened in terror.

"No! No! You can't."

Unmoved, Lisa quickly strode to the chair, slapped Jennifer twice, and sprayed the contents of the bottle into Jennifer's face, forcing her to inhale the substance as she squirmed, unable to escape.

Pointing to her purse, Lisa said, "You better pray to whatever god you currently believe in that your antidote works, because if it doesn't, you're going to see me again, and it won't be nearly as pleasant as this visit."

Jennifer was sobbing, yet I could feel no pity. Her greed and lack of ethics had brought her to this moment.

Lisa looked at me and said, "Let's go."

I nodded assent to Lisa as Jennifer pleaded to know with what she'd been dosed. Lisa remained silent as I replaced the gag and we left the apartment.

•   •   •

Waiting for the elevator to arrive, we both remained silent, staring at the floor indicator. When the elevator arrived and the doors opened, it was vacant, so we stepped aboard, turned around, and waited for the doors to close. As we began our descent, I asked, "Are you OK?"

Lisa, still staring straight ahead at the unmoving doors, said with great enthusiasm, "I'm better than OK. I'm fucking awesome!"

I looked at her, amazed at the response and said, "I have to know, what did you dose her with?"

She finally turned to face me, the grin barely contained on her face. "Nothing. Just plain tap water. I hope she spends the rest of her miserable life trying to figure it out."

I had no words, but stared at my girlfriend in wonder. As the doors opened and we exited the elevator, we were both laughing so hard we could barely walk.

THE END

ACKNOWLEDGEMENTS

Having had a previous novel published, (Warning: Blatant Commercialism Ahead) namely *Watching (A Different Type of Time Travel), Volume 1: The Garden Museum Heist*, got me thinking about the next novel. I know, I should have instantly delved into Volume 2 of the *Watching* series, but I just wasn't ready to go there again so soon. So, while thinking of possible stories, I revisited some previous writings and notes that are stored on my computer, when I came across a screenplay I'd written. I remembered the basics, but reread it for a fresh perspective. I still liked the story! An added bonus was that it had some relevancy to today's world. I made my decision and went about novelizing the screenplay. Doing so is quite a different experience from writing a novel straight from your head, and I learned a lot in the process. I hope you enjoyed reading it as much I did writing it.

As I've said before, a novel does not get written in a vacuum. Once again, I had the support of my wife as I woke in the middle of the night or early morning to either make notes or write based on what I'd just discovered in my head. I wrote and rewrote and she read and reread. Thank you.

And of course, none of this would be possible without Back Rose Writing. Thank you team BRW!

And thank you to my beta readers for providing support and suggestions along the way.

I couldn't have done this without all of you.
Until next time, take care and keep reading!

ABOUT THE AUTHOR

Jeffrey Jay Levin grew up in Chicago, Illinois and, after pestering his wife for 25 years or so, successfully convinced her to move to Northern Arizona, where they currently reside. Jay, as he's known to his friends, spends some time working as a commercial real estate lawyer, and writes whenever he can. He's still working on his customized 1976 Corvette but is hopeful to have it completed by the time his next book is published. In the meantime, he's keeping busy and, mostly, out of trouble.

JEFFREY JAY LEVIN
WATCHING
A DIFFERENT TYPE OF TIME TRAVEL
VOLUME 1
THE GARDEN MUSEUM HEIST

NOTE FROM JEFFREY JAY LEVIN

Word-of-mouth is crucial for any author to succeed. If you enjoyed *Deep Cover*, please leave a review online—anywhere you are able. Even if it's just a sentence or two. It would make all the difference and would be very much appreciated.

Thanks!
Jeffrey Jay Levin

We hope you enjoyed reading this title from:

www.blackrosewriting.com

Subscribe to our mailing list – *The Rosevine* – and receive **FREE** books, daily
deals, and stay current with news about upcoming releases
and our hottest authors.
Scan the QR code below to sign up.

Already a subscriber? Please accept a sincere thank you for being a fan of
Black Rose Writing authors.

View other Black Rose Writing titles at
www.blackrosewriting.com/books and use promo code
PRINT to receive a **20% discount** when purchasing.